CW00516970

Into Her Mother's Eyes

Antonietta Russo

Dear Amanda,
may the light always
shine your way
Amoney

INTO HER MOTHER'S EYES

INTRODUCTION

She could feel notes of an unforgotten melody coming from the radio station, directly from the past. A sound barely audible but noticeably nostalgic, with a particular bitter taste typical only of an era never lived but dreamed and yearned for.

Everything in the room seemed to communicate regularity and normality. The few pictures hanging on the walls with those slightly timid colours were frightened to dare, frightened to show too much security - as if confidence was abolished. Everywhere ruled a neutral beige.

... A newspaper, carelessly left open on an unmade bed. Among its pages, various stories were fighting for attention. There had been a major competition which someone won and someone else would accept the defeat sportingly. Images showed that there would be good weather all week, but as a veiled threat, the weekend seemed to be covered with clouds. And the obligatory horoscope, there to give false hopes to believers in need "love will come, your life will change, and the sun will shine forever, high in the sky: for you, only for you who read this and believe it."

And on that bed, there she was. Sitting there with her legs crossed, arms dangling, and a gaze lost in another dimension. A spacious bed, a big room, a bunch of essential furniture and a single person alone in the centre of everything: Selin... that was her name!

A few weeks ago she past thirty and her existence seemed confused now more than ever. Her eyes as dark as the colour of the night and her mind too busy trying to make its way into the hidden corners of her soul. She thought of the person she was just a few weeks before. A strong, independent woman who had built her place in the world with hard work and sacrifice, and a successful career to show for it. Of the ambitious nature and the specific character, the work had been her only thought: the only aspect of life for which she gave her soul, grit her teeth and would sometimes cry and fall into disarray if the results were not as expected. Having graduated in law at the age of twenty-four with ease, she was able to realise her dream of entering the city's most successful company, Bros & Brothers, through an internship. After which the value, the dedication and the passion she showed had allowed her to stay and fully become a junior lawyer with the prosperous path in front of her growing rapidly. On her thirties she was still working for the same firm and she was now one of the lawyers with the highest success rate for the courtroom cases and the chance to quickly become one of the youngest senior partner of the company. Everything was going as intended. All her goals had been achieved, her dreams realized: a great career in the big city!

Just over a month before, she received a call and nuances which she did not even imagine existed began to emerge around her. Suddenly, so frequently her heart beat at a rate that she did not believe was possible. And now she was left alone in a room too large for such a petite girl lost in an unreal world.

CHAPTER I

It was a Thursday night. She had just returned to her small but cosy house after getting through yet another stressful day in Milan - always hectic, always desperately pursuing some kind of imaginary goal. She loved that crazy world. She savoured the intense energy and felt intoxicated by it at all times. There was nothing better for her than the fury and the passion that the city would communicate. It could transform boring days at the office into crazy and exciting fights for survival. Almost half of her life had been lived among the busy streets and under the grey skies of that city, and never once did she regret it. But there was something really important she had learned from living in a city that was so intense: balance. She enjoyed the hustle of daily life but would find a way to balance it in order to prevent herself from being carried away with it all and collapse. That's why she created habits that helped her to relax, release the tensions of the day and prepare for the next challenge. And Selin had found that balance. The atmosphere changed for her the moment she passed through the door of her flat. That was the moment in which the world was no longer granted the privilege of breaking into that calm so hardly conquered. The chaos was no longer a welcome guest in her home. The door closed and the usual ritual finally began. Shoes rigorously removed in the entrance and gently placed against one side of the door; handbag dropped, not too gently, on that small table immediately located on her right hand side designed for the express purpose of containing all the junks that she needed to carry around during the day. And then, through the living room and the bedroom, directly into the bathroom where hot water and scented soaps would soon fill up the pearly bathtub - that was her secret corner.

And while the water flowed gracefully, this little room began to fill with a light vapour that would inevitably steam up her reading glasses which she wore throughout the day, definitely out of necessity but also because it gave her that look of a mature and adult person. A look that her delicate and soft features always prevent her from having. Even today at the not-so-tender age of twenty-nine, almost thirty, she could not walk into a store to buy a bottle of wine without being asked to show an identity document. At the thought, as always, a smile suddenly came up to adorn her face. Of course, every time that happened she would get annoyed, especially when she would forget to carry her ID. But when she reflected back on it in the evening, with her glass of rosé wine held tight in her hands, the fresh taste on her lips and the warmth in her body, that's when the smile yes would appear on her face. And slowly, one by one, she would began to light all the candles in shades of dark green, her favourite colour: a reminder of wild nature. Those candles were all over the bath ... and the sink, and on the mirror, and on the shoe rack, and clothes hamper. Everywhere! Luckily for her, the candles were an inexpensive purchase or she would have burned through all of her salary in no time. But before diving in the tub there was still one thing she had to do. The finishing touch for perfection: the rapid and final race in the kitchen, where a bottle of rosé wine was waiting to share its fruity flavour with her lips. Having poured a single glass of wine, the right amount to relax her muscles from the high voltage of her everyday life without suffering negative side effects, Selin came back into the bathroom where she placed the glass on the edge of the tub now full of foam. She freed herself of her clothes, piece by piece, falling on the surrounding floor. Slow and soft on her skin, messily left on the ground. She knew that after her yearned bath she would end up putting those clothes in the dirty clothes basket nearby. But now her only thought was to totally immerse herself in that hot, frothy water: in a room lit only by the timid flame given off by candles, a single glass of rosé wine on her bathtub and those delicate bubbles that inebriated her.

Just before submerging completely in the tub, she would press the 'ON' button on the small stereo purposely placed on a table in the corner of the room: graceful notes of a forgotten piece of classical music began to float in the air, slow and then fast, then slow once again. That unique and magical sound given off by a piano where expert and confident fingers glided effortlessly between the various buttons, letting the air fill up with poetry and magic.

And so without waiting any further, and a naked leg after the other, her body slid into a different dimension, warm, cosy, protective - a perfect dimension that nothing and no one could dent. Even her own thoughts were silent. Her mind, usually filled with noise, sank with the rest of her body in that moment of peace and the only sounds accepted were the notes of Beethoven, representing the background of an imaginary paradise. No other sound was audible, not the noise of the crowds and city traffic, not the child's crying who lived in the apartment above her and certainly not the barking of dogs from the street or the television blaring somewhere in her building which seemed like a mandatory requirement.

After only ten minutes, in the distance, you could hear another sound that did not belong to the specificity of the moment. A shrill sound, metallic, arrogant, aggressive - one ring after another the phone continued to make its presence felt in a desperate but futile attempt to interrupt her peace. Selin would ignore the shrill sound firstly because, she would not let anyone thwart that wonderful moment and, secondly, she knew all too well whom it was. The same person that tried to contact her all day and, tired of being neglected by mobile had also taken the liberty to call her in her workplace where she declined herself once again. And, then, knowing her schedule, she now tried to call her at home. Of course it was her mother. Over time her mother had become increasingly possessive and intrusive. She could certainly understand that living so far apart and with the possibility to see each other only twice a year, and only for a few days each time, was a difficult situation to accept. But instead of getting used to the idea by now, after many years away, her mother had begun to do the opposite. If one day she forgot to call her, she knew that the next day she would have faced a telephone conversation of at least thirty minutes where the first twenty-nine were characterised by constant complaints about Selin not loving her. That after have given her birth, looking after her and have made sacrifices for her, her daughter simply ignored her.

Only in the last minute of the conversation would she remembered to ask, "But tell me my daughter, how are you?". Their relationship had never been good. For some reason they never understood each other. They were too different and Selin had accepted that. This was one of the reasons why she had left her home town, Bernalda, at the first chance she got. She liked nothing about that life, or better yet, there was nothing in that life which she could feel in harmony with.

As opposed to Milan, where she could feel that she belonged. But her mother did not seem to grasp all those basic clues that she gave her constantly. Incessantly, her mother tried to rehabilitate a bridge between them that was simply never built. In recent weeks then it had worsened. Her mother had arranged a family dinner, a kind of reunion to regain all of her children together in the same room after years that various life commitments had made them leave toward other places on the planet. Selin wondered why her mother was so nostalgic for that time. And yet she was still a young woman, in her fifties with a busy social life and a husband who continued to look at her with adoring eyes as if they were always at the beginning of their love story. Selin often wondered if she will ever have the same luck: the luck of experiencing that feeling of being loved unconditionally. That feeling of being considered more important that the very act of breathing? She wondered... but she was also aware that she had given too much to her job to ever be able to create space for a partner, let alone a family. However, her mother wanted her children close by and believed that dinner was the means to make that happen. Her mother had asked all of them to take a few days off from work to spend time together in the small southern town that had been her home for her first eighteen years. Although she had said yes, her mother was afraid that she would change her mind at the last moment and that, using her work as an excuse, she would avoid dinner. Among other things, certainly she could not blame her. It would not be the first time that such a thing happened. Having always put career ahead of everything and everyone, any kind of unexpected event, deadline or setback of any kind or degree in the workplace was always her priority. And there she was, at the last moment, calling her parents to cancel the trip because "work was always first and foremost." This time she knew she could not. Her mother had put in a lot of effort to organize this family dinner and for once she wanted to try not to disappoint her. But more than anything she liked the idea of spending a few days with her siblings, back to being a little younger, just to break that sense of responsibility that the constant living alone in such a big city with so many obligations and duties involved. And more than anything, there was nothing in the world worth seeing her mother full of rage over this dinner organised months in advance, take the train and break into her dear Milan. That was her reality and her mother was not a member of it and, even more so, she did not want her to be. The status quo of her existence satisfied her a lot. She let the hot frothy water wash away all of her thoughts, let the musical notes burst into her mind and drown any concern, let the delicate flavour of the wine give warmth to her body and the soft light of candles melt away her weary eyes. And, in this state, without even realizing it, she fell into a brief, deep, dreamless sleep as if nothing more was real. Nor her house, nor her body, nor her thoughts. Pure nothingness.

She woke up suddenly an hour later, the water cold, the music finished, the foam disappeared and the faint glimmer of a few candles that stoically struggled against the darkness. Disappointed by the unexpected awakening, she pushed herself up using her arms for leverage and got out of the tub feeling numb in the entirety of her body. Once out of the tub she quickly grabbed a towel and wrapped it around her cold and wet body. And, once again, suddenly the sound of the telephone pierced her ears and her thoughts and only then she realized that was that same sound that had awoken her from her deep sleep. While still wet and protected from nudity with just a towel she walked into the living room to answer the phone aware that this torture would never end as long as she had not accepted the inevitable hour of agony. She wanted to avoid falling asleep again, this time in a comfortable bed, and be brutally brought back to reality by that sound.

"Hello!" She said with a tone not too friendly.

"You realize that I tried to contact you all day and not once have you answered me. NOT ONCE! I was beginning to think that they had kidnapped you, taken you to a cold, dark cellar, a sort of bunker where you were unable to use the phone. Because this is the only acceptable explanation to your total disregard of the concerns of a mother. Not once, not twice ... but at least twenty times I tried to call today. And you... nothing! Do you think I would have called so many times if it was not important? If you just think of all the sacrifices I made for you. Is this the way to thank me? But I suppose the idea of thanking me is not even going through your mind. That's the problem of today's young generation: so selfish, so quick to demand and to take everything for granted ... everything is owed. But it's my fault, I educated you badly. I have loved you too much and I forgave you when I should have given you a few slaps instead."

Considering to herself her mother had tried to call her nearly fifty times that day, not twenty as she claimed, she took a long breath. Just as she expected, her mother, as usual, did not even feel the need to introduce herself when answering the phone but rather get straight to the point: with her criticism or the latest gossip of the town or updates about her sisters and brother. The topic was not as important as the fact that it had to be immediately told! Without dwelling on unnecessary preambles such as "Hello darling, it's your mother. How are you?" That would be a waste of time. Now she knew she had to stop her, had to say something if she wanted to avoid going crazy and be infected by her neurosis. She knew that her mother could continue for months. She knew very well that if she would not stop her immediately, Selin would have had a headache at the end of the phone call and would feel strangely infected by her anger indefinitely.

"Mum, you're right. I am irresponsible as usual. And yet you know that I do not want personal calls at work. As I've already said, sometimes I'm not able to call for a day or two and there's not need to make a big deal about it!"

"Oh, but we both know the truth. You are avoiding me just because you do not have the courage to tell me that this weekend you will not be here. Well now, I know you my dear daughter! But I do not care. You can build any excuse you like. Should the sun not rise from the east, you'll still be here Friday night to spend the weekend together and have dinner together and for once after years and years we will be a real family. Lately, I seem to not have any children. Even people on the street have begun to doubt whether I really have children.

And, how could I argue with them: I never see you, we just talk on the phone and now you want to avoid even calling me. How could you do that?"

By now her mother was a raging river. Unstoppable, like a waterfall that relentlessly continued its violent run and, endlessly, without fear, continued to break against the hard rock.

"I have already arranged everything, all your brothers have confirmed and will be here tomorrow. And we will spend time together whether you like it or not."

"But Mum I have confirmed too."

"Selin, don't take it in the wrong way but I must say that when it comes to family your word is worth very little. This time you must know you would not only disappointing me, everyone here will be disappointed too. And I still cannot comprehend how you can put your damn job ahead of your own blood. I have tolerated it in the past but I cannot justify it any longer. Not at this time. Selin, we actually need to talk. I'm so worried about you. The life you're living, the future that you're not building, there's so much we have to say." She spoke with an enthusiasm and a nostalgic note that was new to the cauldron of her complaints.

"There's no reason to worry about my life. I have proven several times that I'm able to survive alone. I do not understand what you mean!"

"We really need to talk and you have to promise to call me more often in the months ahead; they will be difficult for everyone."

Tired of hearing her mum complaining, Salin said, "You are right mum, I have to call you more often and I'll try... seriously! And for the weekend, do not worry, I'll come home and we will have all the time you want to talk, during which you will be able to reproach me for all the ills of the world, if you want. If it makes you feel better, I told everyone that I'm going to turn my phone off for the whole weekend and that they will have to sort it out any last minute emergency on their own. Are you happy?"

"And you will not make up any excuses?" her mother said imploringly

"Actually, I've NEVER invented any excuse. There were always some serious unexpected events that emerged at work. Anyway, Mum, no, no excuses for this weekend. All your children will be there with you and we will give you so much torment that you will not want to see us all together for the rest of your existence." Selin said in a slightly ironic tone to try to break the tension that had arisen, and was now also noticeable on the phone.

"Can I really count on you to be here?" Insisted her mother with her sceptical tone 'I've seen far too many things in my life to be able to trust'.

"Mum don't worry" and after a slight pause to give her time to digest what had been said, "Now I have to say goodbye mum. I had to jump out of the tub to answer you, and I have not had time to dry. So unless you want me to cancel the flight back home because of a common flu, I would say that this is the time to say goodbye."

"Okay, okay dear, go ahead, go ahead! Dry thoroughly. See you soon."

"See you soon, mum... but wait, before you said that there was something important that you had to tell me and that was the reason why you have tried to contact me so many times," although in her mind she knew that she would still try to contact her billions of times without having to be very important or rather, not at all important.

"No, no. Don't worry, do not think about it, I just wanted to see if you were coming. A big kiss and go get dry so that you don't get sick. See you tomorrow!"

"Goodbye mother, goodbye."

As Selin predicted, there it was! A torture lasted an entire day just to know if she was still heading home or not ... unbelievable! Her mother really had a unique ability to torture her mentally. She hung up, and could not help but think of her mother's voice when greeting her, which was so strangely full of pain and suffering. But perhaps it was just a supposition. Maybe she was simply devising new techniques to leverage her guilt, the black sheep of the family. The daughter who had not devoted herself to the family, that for many years didn't need advice or suggestions of any kind from her family, that survives perfectly without them. She abandoned those thoughts and went into the bedroom, put on her comfortable pyjamas and went to bed.

She wonder why her preference was always for loose pyjamas that were three size too big. Since she was a teenager she had this habit. She could wear all those tiny, body wrapping clothes during the day but at night she needed to feel free; her body did not want to feel the shackles. And with this simple and slightly silly thought, she became enveloped by the soft weight of the sheets and fell asleep. She had troubled dreams. Tormented, clear skies that made room for dark clouds from which protruded lightning and thunder. The country house of her father, always deeply loved by her, was split in two and gave way to a crater from which flowed out high and threatening flames. And smoke rose up into the sky and covered the entire surrounding area. A sudden gust of wind stirred the smoke and she could finally find herself, terrified, on the brink. She had a bad feeling that she was about to collapse - she wanted to collapse. Tormented, she saw herself jump into the flames, towards nothing. She woke up in a cold sweat, with her heart pounding and a sense of overwhelming loss. It took her quite a while to calm down and realize that she was in her room and she was safe. Nothing bad was really happening. It was only a bad dream. She turned on the light and looked at the time on the phone: it was just quarter past two. She knew she would have to wake up very early the next day, just as she knew that it would not be easy to go back to sleep with that sense of uneasiness invading her. She got back under the covers but she could not find the courage to turn off the lamp that night. She turned on the television on which a documentary about animals gave her company until her eyes softly closed and by three in the morning finally, she fell asleep.

CHAPTER II

The next day she got up very early, around six in the morning, to have enough time to pack her bags before going to work. But there was still that sense of agitation, from the previous night, that she felt vividly and she could not understand what was happening to her. It was so long since she had nightmares. Or maybe not... usually she could not remember her dreams. Was it possible that the conversation with her mother had indisposed her so much that it even influenced her dreamlike activity? And anyway, since when did she take into consideration anything her mother said to her? However, she knew that now it was morning and the morning meant concentration and organisation. As usual there was a lot to do. First of all the luggage: she was going to spend only three days or so in her home town. She had already booked her return flight for Sunday evening so there was no need to carry too much with her.

A couple of bras and pants, two pairs of socks, a dress, a pair of trousers and two pairs of shirts. Her dress style was always very classic wherever she was. And that is because she wanted to always feel ready to see a client, to attend a meeting, to meet with the counterpart or for any unforeseen event that should ever arise... she was always ready.

Salin flew that same day, straight after work. She had already booked a taxi that was going to pick her up from work at 5.30p.m. and take her to the bus station. And a few hours later she would be in the cosy arms of her family - or at least she hoped so. She planned to take the luggage with her to work, so she decided to only prepare one piece of hand luggage which would be more than enough for her needs. After all, it was just a weekend. And, moreover, her sisters were also going to be there which would give her access to a very big wardrobe indeed. Lots of clothes to be exchanged. It was inevitable. So in the end it was like having a double wardrobe, or one three times bigger in this case. It had always been like that and always would be! Certainly her sisters style was far from her own but for just a weekend she could adapt. Selin has two sisters and a brother.

One of the sisters, Amaia, was only two and a half years older than her but they could not have been more different. In fact, they were polar opposites. Amaia was her second mother. Thirty-two years old, married for six years to her first and only high school love with whom she had grown up. Passionate about history, she graduated with honours in ancient languages and literatures with the secret dream of becoming a teacher. But she had never been ambitious and had always believed deeply in the value of family which she always put first, unlike Selin. So after graduating, Amaia and Federico, the only love of her life, began to organize their wedding celebrations for the following year. And so six years and two children later, was the only one to have remained in the same town as their parents and the only one to have prioritised her love for family over her true passion for ancient literature and for teaching.

In the end however, she found a way to teach by offering herself as a volunteer to help elementary school children, with the after-school program. And sometimes even during the summer organizing specialized courses or retakes for kids a little older. Whatever the need, she was there to help. She was very active in the community as well, and the thing that had always shocked Selin was that it was all for free, never once did she ask to be paid. She saw it as a way to meet different kids, at home or at school - it was not important - and to let her own children socialize in a safe environment. And the rewards were plentiful. Other parents always brought a gift to thank her, such as fresh fruit just harvest from the countryside or home-made cakes and biscuits. But most of all, what made her happy was that her children were well regarded and they were always invited to birthday parties or football matches. This was how important her family was to her. And most of all, Amaia was really happy with the choice she made and no one had ever heard her regret the sacrifices made. Not once. Her ability to teach and transmit love joint with her patience and her infinite capacity to listen had made her a perfect mother, the backbone of a strong and united family. And with her marriage still intact and the children happy, she knew she had made the right choice and there was nothing to regret.

Slightly younger than her, with just over a year between them was Stefano, her little brother who she loved deeply. Beautiful and incredibly sure of himself, he was a classic womaniser. Tall, dark, eyes dark as night, had always had the charm of beautiful and damned especially since a few years before, her sisters had told him he would be the perfect man if only he grew a hint of a beard. And he had heard ... this falsely perfect unkempt beard did grow to make him the most handsome man in the world, especially for his sisters. Stefano, of his great passion for women had never made a secret, as he had never made any secret of his total disregard for books and study and all it would go near.

After struggling to finish high school, he clearly expressed no intention of wasting even a single extra minute of his time on university books. And the only reason why he got to the end of the high school was because forced by his parents and sisters to take the degree behind horrific threats against his manhood. The problem was that besides the women, there was nothing that impassioned him. He had no vocation. So as a natural consequence he started travelling which his parents had to agree to as long as he was able to pay for his irresponsibility on his own and did not ask them to finance it. Italy, Germany, Austria, England, Switzerland... every three or four months he would feel bored and decide to change nationality in search of new excitement. Unfortunately for his parents, they could never reproach him for the choices made because from the very beginning he made himself self sufficient. Wherever he went, he immediately found a new job all by itself thanks to his undeniable charm. He tried it all, from working in restaurants, in the kitchen or as a gardener, in factories as an employee or in a cleaning company. He always found something within a few days of his arrival in the new city. Independent and proud, even in the brief moments of difficulty, he had never wanted to ask anyone for help.

And then, two years before, his wanderings seemed to have stopped when he arrived in Barcelona, and decided to open his own bar near the beach. Apparently, without saying anything to anyone, during the years as a globe-trotter he had managed to save up some money while waiting to find his calling. The city of Barcelona was for him the woman he still had not been able to fall deeply in love with and offer his total dedication. Within a few days of his arrival to the city he decided that this was the place where he wanted to be. The beach, the culture, the colours, and the joy of the place, all fascinated him. He took advantage of his big experience in hospitality to open his own place. Small and cosy, it was immediately a hit. Customers never lack and his way of doing so pleasant and intriguing meant that people had always wanted to make their return again and again. Only months before, she had a chance to take a few days of vacation to visit her brother and see for herself if he was really well or not, and after one quick look, she realised that her brother was now a businessman, a grown man who knew how to get through just fine in that crazy world. Selin found herself repeatedly thinking about the fact that if only Stefano had wanted to study a little more, he could have become anyone he wanted. He would even have become a much better lawyer than her and with half the effort. No jury would ever resist him and that was for sure. He was now a perfect man. Still a womaniser, but with his head on his shoulders.

And then there was her Arianna, the baby of the family, who was born after a long break of seven years. Her parents had taken a while to decide whether or not have a last child but they definitely put a lot of love into it: Arianna was the most beautiful of all, full of energy and will to live, she spent her days running from one place to another always with something to do. Her unstoppable joy and vitality meant that she was always surrounded by friends who loved a lot of good.

Arianna knew how to be loved. Her passion for art, fashion and the beauty of the world in general, had led her to first do a fashion course in Paris and then a photography course in London where she now resided and from which from time to time, she sent all the family photos of the most absurd, crazy and beautiful kind Salin had ever seen. Her sister really had the ability to make everything she touched and photographed unique. But she still remembered the photo that moved her most of all. The one of her first year in Paris, her first year of the fashion course. Arianna, with a most dazzling smile, holding in her hands with such pride and happiness the first dress designed and made entirely by her. Everyone knew from then on that her life would be among the most magical fairy tales ever told.

Selin loved all of her siblings unconditionally, all so different from each other but all so wonderful. She always tried to keep in touch as much as possible, to call or, when they could, arrange to meet again. Often she happened to feel deeply the absence of her siblings and thought how it would be nice to live all together in one place, but their aspirations and their characters were so different that the thought alone would not have been allowed. Anyway, being away had never stopped them loving each other more at every moment. At first it was not easy, especially for their parents, having to accept to see each of their children separately leave their home, their shelter but their parents would not have expected anything less. Since they were children, they had all been encourage to have an amount of energy that a small village such as theirs could never encompass. While deciding what to pack, Selin could not hold back the happiness of seeing for the first time, maybe after ten years, her siblings all together under one roof. She felt nostalgic.

Honestly, who knew how many more years would pass before such an opportunity was going to come again. With this in mind she decided that she would have enjoyed as much as possible that living once again in her parents' home, the home where she had been child and joyful. She imagined that she would probably have argued with her mother because she cooked too much fried food and accepted the scolding that her father gave her because he loved her and wanted to show her how things worked in this difficult life and how things were very different in his time, as if she were still thirteen. Who knows, she might have told some tale to her niece and nephew and exchanged secrets with her sisters at night, lights off, to avoid being discovered by the parents and avoid prying ears and finally, she would chased her brother through the house because he stole a bra and was waving it around the whole house just to the satisfaction of seeing his sister blushing.

Yes, she missed it all! She missed that chaos that represented her family. She packed the small amount needed for a family weekend and left her apartment ready to catch the underground to get to work but impatient to get back to feeling like a child again, even if only for two and a half days.

The day was intense as usual. Friday in any other office usually meant starting to relax and getting ready for the weekend, but not there. In their firm there was always so much to do and most of them would simply never leave. She was not the only one to take home the documents and continue to work on a Friday evening.

Some of her colleagues, who had a shared house with other people, even decided to return to work in the studio overnight to escape the noise. She had to notify Gabriele, her boss, way in advance that she could not take over extra duties for those two days and, time to time, remind him of it to avoid the surprise "I didn't know anything about that". He was a strong and determined man, whom built that firm from scratch and turned it in the most prestigious firm in town. Although never forcing anyone's hand to work beyond their agreed times, everyone knew that he was expecting the best - he expected success. Among other things, Gabriele paid very well, and offered good incentives so all of them could feel constantly motivated to give more. Almost no surprise when, shooting her suitcase and ready to leave work, Selin saw Gabriele fall upon a fury in the office, over-excited "We did it! We got him! Do you remember the case of that car accident in which you made the first interview three days ago? The wealthy businessman, what was his name?"

"You mean Mr. Rossi?"

"Yes him. He just called me saying he's been impressed by your professionalism and knowledge in the industry and has decided to ask our firm to pursue his case. Isn't that fantastic?"

"It is fantastic news. Monday morning I will contact him and I will start to prepare him for his first deposition."

"Monday... are you kidding? He wants you to go to his house now, he wants to talk and see if he can really trust us. This guy will pay a lot of money, you do not understand. If we win this case, he will use us for the rest of his life."

Only when Selin turned a worried look down he realized that there was also a suitcase in that room "Where the hell do you think you're going?!"

"Gabriele it's been a month now that I've reminded you constantly that this weekend I am not available. As I've told you a hundred times, I'm going to visit my family in the South and have a flight leaving in exactly four hours. So now I'm going at the airport."

"Man, I forgot. This is a problem. He wants to see you now, he will not wait until Monday."

"I'll call him while I'm in the taxi and explain that I had previous commitments and that I can not meet him now. And, if he wants me to explain something to him I can already do that on the phone."

"No... no..." Gabriele began to agitate his index in the air as he did whenever a sudden idea struck him "four hours ... it's perfect," he tapped the palms of the hands against each other with an excessive enthusiasm "the client's house is on the road to the airport. Go to his house, see him, be there for half an hour and no more and then you will still have time to catch your flight. I am sending you a message with his address," and so, he turned and walked out hastily from Selin's office so completely ignoring the last sentence that she tried to argue "but you know that it can take hours to organize a client statement..." Words lost in the wind.

Selin felt trapped. With a quick look at her watch and a profanity whispered through clenched teeth she grabbed the suitcase, rushed out of the studio and jumped in the first available taxi. Twenty minutes later she was at Mr. Rossi's house. She was not even sure she could call it a house - it looked more like a miniature castle. She left her suitcase in the taxi and asked the taxi driver to wait for her so that he could take her directly to the airport after. That trip was going to cost her a fortune, she thought. She had exactly thirty minutes of spare time. She could do it, she just had to be as clear and concise as possible. Selin composed herself and rang the bell.

"Mr. Rossi, I'm really happy to see you again" Selin dressed her most dazzling smile and her professional nature took over. "How are you today? Have you started to recover from the trauma?"

"My head still hurts sometimes, but I always feel better when I think that bastard is going to pay generously for having my car scratched." And that was it: a scratch on the car. But people from Milan knew how to be very vindictive and very rich and her law firm loved that kind of customer.

"Do not worry, my office will ensure that you're compensated more than adequately. Now, on Monday afternoon we will have our first meeting with the lawyer of the other party. We will analyse the facts and try first to reach a civil settlement. We'll see what they offer and, if we are happy with it, we will not go to court."

"I want that asshole to give away his own underwear," interrupted Mr. Rossi.
"And we will help you do this. Let me explain in general terms how this meeting will take place."

Keeping a mental calculation of time passing Selin guided him through the meeting structure and potential obstacles that could emerge

"But consider that even though you are going to be there, it's up to us lawyers to argue. We want this meeting to take place in the most civilized way possible and not leave any chance of mistaken words that could get you less than you deserve. Is that clear?"

"Sure, sure."

"Now try to enjoy the weekend and do not speak with anyone about the accident without my presence. We will meet again Monday. I will come to pick you up at lunch time to eat together and brush up on guidelines and from there I will take over." said Selin as she began to get up from the chair.

"But are you already going away? Don't you even want a coffee?" replied dryly Mr. Rossi.

"I'd really like to but I'm going to a charity dinner, a very informal gala and restricted to a few tens of people working in the field of the legislature. There will be many judges, including those who will follow your case if we decide to end up in court" Selin lied shamelessly.

"I like to act in advance and be ready for anything. Having friends in the right places is what secures the win, right?"

"I like the way you think, lawyer" said Mr. Rossi squeezing her hand and accompanying her to the door. "I wish you a wonderful evening," he greeted her with a wink.

"See you on Monday," she said without looking back. She was proud of this great lie with which not only had she managed to escape from there in a mere twenty-five minutes, but that had allowed her to earn complete respect and trust from her new client. She slipped into the taxi, finally, heading directly to the airport, hoping that there were not going to be other obstacles in the way.

Just outside of Bari airport, she realized soon that was now close to home that the typically southern warmth was not just the family environment nearing, but also the climate. There could be another glacial age in the rest of the world, but there in the South of Italy you could feel nothing but warmth. A warmth that would melt anyone heart away. Although she had to be honest with herself and admit that the tenderness of the air of the South was strongly opposed by the uselessness of public transport. Reminding herself that she was not a patient person, she went to buy a magazine and prepared herself to wait a full hour before being able to get into the only available bus that would eventually take her home. The last bit of wait before to be hug by friendly arms. She would gladly have called a taxi to avoid that wait. Since she began to work, and consequently to gain money, she had always got everything she wanted without wasting time on unnecessary waiting or without getting overwhelmed by unfulfilled desires. Unfortunately, the South did not offer such a wide range of choice in transportation. There was only a certain train or a certain bus at any given time and you had to be okay with that and the taxis? Rare pearls in those endless landscapes.

But it was fine. Now she only came home once or twice a year so she could accept it. In addition, she had long since realised that every place had its strengths and its flaws and that the southern beauties were such as to make you forget any limits you could have! As she sipped her cappuccino and read her magazine she decided to call her mother once again to calm her down, tell her the flight went well and to anticipate some of the delicacies that she would cook for them! She knew she would put on weight in those two days but could not wait to get the big binge. After all, her mother was an incredible talent in the kitchen. In just two hours, Selin could confirm her memories of her mother's skill. She was the last sibling to arrive. The others had already arrived in the afternoon and after large and warm embraces, they were all set to enjoy the first family dinner together after years.

Their home was really great. Nothing like those tiny spaces that you paid so much for in the north! Most of the houses in the south were really large, with several floors and countless rooms. Furthermore her home had a special meaning. It had been built seventy years earlier by her grandfather, the father of her father. And thanks to the love that her father and mother always showed in its daily maintenance, the house was still full of splendour and vigour! From the entrance there were stairs going down and the other that went upwards. Going down you found the wine cellar, a her father's favourite - his pride and joy. He kept all the bottles of wine that he produced himself. The countryside was his passion. He cultivated all kinds of plants and among them a large part of it was dedicated to his vineyard. Olive and orange trees also thrived in its spacious grounds. Not to mention the small plot dedicated to tomatoes, lettuce, cabbage, green beans and more, use for her parent's daily sustenance. One thing that her mother was never tired of telling her children about was the authenticity of this products and how leaving the small town they had stopped eating properly. They could eat up to ten meals a day but that was not to be called food. It was just something chemically composed for mass production. Just fake tastes for city people. It was something that was polluting their bodies from within. The truth was that Selin had never been able to deny anything her mother said on that subject because she knew that the only way to do would be lying. The truth was that there was nothing comparable to the delicate flavour of vegetables eaten immediately after being collected which did not receive any special treatment other than that which the nature had to offer: a warm sun, the damp earth, so much water and her father's love. Every time Selin went to the countryside, she loved to collect the delicate fruit from trees and eat them. She loved fill her belly with real, tasteful oranges. She had to admit to herself that she missed the times when children organized picnics in the countryside and she would kick a ball around with her siblings between meals and all together they would helped their father to pick fruits and vegetables. The thing she liked best was to collect oranges because every time she took an orange in her hand, her father's words came to mind. He taught her the technique: rotate the wrist, bend the hand, and then again turn and bend. She did not understand why but that movement was both funny and reassuring at the same time. She also liked picking grapes, but when she was little, her mother was always too scared to let her use scissors and over time Selin had stopped try. Although over the years, one after the other, all of the children had stopped helping him, their father continued to take care of his countryside, his vineyard and his wine that would occupy a place of honour in his father's cellar every year.

Up a few steps was the immense living room where her mother loved to spend his afternoons in the company of her friends and neighbours, or, when she wasn't waiting for guests, to stretch out on the couch with the television on and take a nap. The living room, like the rest of the house, had classic and simple furnishings: wood furniture and walls in soft tones. On the walls were paintings of abstract content, made by her younger sister. For after all, whilst their mother could openly criticize their choices in life, in reality she could not be more proud. And Arianna, with her particular talent in all that could be labelled as art, occupied a special place in her mother's heart. From the lively and slightly cheeky character she knew how to conquer the hardest heart. Her mother did not express her pride easily and loudly, at least not directly to hers children, but she proved with facts. So although she had always said that art was not a job and at best a hobby, her daughter refused to listen and follow her advice and her paintings were now covering most of the walls of their home.

On the left a long corridor led to the bathroom and various bedrooms: the first and smallest belonged to her brother; the second largest where the three siblings shared their secrets in the dark of the night, and finally the biggest and most beautiful belonged to their parents. With a neat and refined touch, it always communicated its grandeur compared to the other two rooms, usually thrown into disorder and chaos, with the doors always open, cupboards and clothes scattered everywhere and a lot of soft toys that were to fill the little free floor space that books and clothes had already taken possession of. Shelves and chairs and then some more shoes: dozens and dozens of shoes everywhere. She had to admit that when she set foot in the room that weekend, she did not recognize it at first. So tidy and organized with only the essentials now inside. It did not correspond with the vague but reassuring memory that she had pictured. Luckily the three sisters together easily brought the mess back in the room: opened their suitcases, threw their clothes and shoes on the bed and on the floor and behold. The house was home again. Even Amaia, the only sister who was still living in their home town had decided after a strong and determined suggestion by her mother to pack her bags and leave her husband and children alone for two days and be a daughter herself again for those two days.

Finally, mother's kingdom was upstairs where an immense kitchen occupied all the space with everything she needed to cook sweet and savoury, from appetizers to main courses, from meat to dessert, whatever she needed could be found in that kitchen. All day, every day, smells of all kinds but always delicious, filled the air. Her mother spent every morning in her kingdom organizing lunch and dinner. Every day could create something new and tantalizing able to water anyone's mouth. Selin had always thought that her mother should write a cookbook. She was not only good, she really had an enviable talent. She could put together the most absurd flavours but in the end it would always be a spectacular dish.

And next to the kitchen an incredibly large terrace where in the cool summer evenings she adored to prepare a dinner for the family before they all abandoned the house to go out with their friends. Each part of the house contained some incredible memories: laughter, confusion, discussions. It was her home!

That Friday all the siblings arrived at different times and everyone wanted to eat something quickly without being a burden. With this in mind their mother had arranged dinner for the following night and everyone knew that they should not make commitments. But that night they were free; free to rediscover their Bernalda, free to visit their former friends, free to be teenagers again. The siblings knew that the following night would give them time to talk about everything but the Friday night was for them. And so, she swallowed a quick bite and after a fast shower and screaming "bye mum, bye dad" she rushed downstairs, slamming the door behind them and, all taking different directions, the siblings went to see their various friends, childhood friends. One of the few remaining ties with that village now distant in time and space. Only Amaia was understandably at home and kept her parents company. She could see her friends every day and certainly did not need to take advantage of those rare and fleeting moments.

Selin did not have to go far, Stella lived just two blocks away. The two of them had known each other since they were only three years old in kindergarten. They came to grow together and do everything together: partners in and out of school. In high school, they began to choose different paths. In fact, both had opted for high school, but while on the one hand Stella chose the village school, Selin had begun to realize that there was something inside her, a push that made her dream of a world outside the little reality of her small town. So after endlessly begging her mother, she began to attend high school, but in the nearby city in their province, Matera, that for her had the air of freedom, and the distance from the family, always a bit too big, a bit too present.

The bus journey to school was only thirty minutes - thirty minutes that for Selin meant a taste of freedom. A little escape that only few years later turned in the greatest escape of all - Milan -. It was not yet the great existential revolution that she hoped to reach, but it was a start, a small crack that allowed her to take a look at what the world was once she abandoned the painting of gracious serenity and accepted coexistence which for her was that tiny village. This had not caused any hitch in their friendship because they continued to see each other every night and often studied together having virtually all the same school subjects to prepare. And the weekend was spent at the house of one or the other in the armchairs by the fireplace to share their dreams and their future projects. Selin had pretty clear ideas. Her plans were to go away from that small town that made her feel suffocated and become a successful woman. Stella instead resembled Selin's older sister more. She dreamed of a family, dreamed of a home, a safe and quiet place: she wanted to be a wife and a mother. The work was not her priority and ambitions were not haunted. A job as a secretary was all Stella needed. It was indeed one of the jobs she searched for.

Becoming older meant that they spent their Saturday night in some pub eating pizza and drinking beer. Even university had failed to move them away. Stella had decided not to continue their studies, and remained in the village, where she started to seek a job and a husband. Selin moved to Milan straight away where she enrolled in law and began her career. Of course things were different. They no longer had the opportunity to see each other as often; indeed, they could hardly see each other at all. Now they met only a few times a year and it was Stella who usually went to visit her in Milan, although she had never made any secret of her contempt for that city for which she though was so cold and inhospitable. But they called each other at least once a week and updated each other on everything that happened in their lives. Their friendship had never been cracked in any way. They had grown and changed together and there was always acceptance toward any change that happen in their lives and in their personality as they grew older. One thing the two friend shared in common was men. Neither of them had been able to sustain a relationship that was worthy of being considered as such!

Stella had risen to find a job as secretary in a private paediatric clinic and she had been working in the same role for eight years now. Because she never got married she preferred not to invest in a home and instead occupy her parents' house. She did not care too much because all her brothers had gone away and her old parents preferred to be on the ground floor. In practice she was equipped to transform the top floor into her own home with the advantage of not having to pay either rent or a mortgage. Her hobbies were the gym and husband's hunting. By now her idea of hunting for a husband was to go clubbing every weekend and hooking up with every cute boy she found. She was a living example of kissing all the toads before finding her prince. And knowing the little village mentality all too well, every weekend she went to town, away from prying eyes to enjoy a weekend of 'beauty & sex' as she loved to call it. Somehow she had decided to spend what she earn in beauty salons and weekends at luxury hotels.

Selin, despite being open minded, tended to be more cautious and distrustful of men. And, above all, they were not her priority. She always needed to know a little, at least a bit, about the person sitting next to her before going into bed and still somehow had the feeling of starting a relationship. Sex without a meaning had never being of any interest for her.

That weekend Stella had remained in town waiting for her and when Selin arrived to her house she did not even have to ring the bell. Waiting for her on the balcony, Stella cried out to her and rushed down the stairs, completely skipping the last steps. They hugged each other with the intense usual enthusiasm and remained so at least for ten minutes screaming, jumping and rejoicing together. Then they entered the warm house and began to tell and to catch up on the latest events. Nothing had changed, it was so easy for them to still be friends. Although physically and mentally they were totally different from when they were young, the affection was still intact. They talked and talked and a bottle of red wine led to the them happily spending the next several hours doing so. At one point, Selin said "Do you have some idea of what's going on with my mother? She is so weird lately! She is crazier than usual; she's very stressing and overwhelming with everyone. Maybe there is some gossip in town that can help me understand. In recent weeks there has been no time when I didn't want to fight with her."

"Oh my darling I have not the faintest idea. If I had heard anything about your mother I would have told you right away, you know! Honestly. And actually I was starting to think also that it was quite strange, it is at least a couple of months since I saw her in the village or let me taste some of her new dessert. You know I love your mother. She's like a mother to me. I know that you two don't have a great relationship but for me she is an exceptional person. Especially since you left the village she virtually adopted me and started to take care of me more than my own parents have ever done! But for two months now I have not heard from her and I'm ashamed to say it, but with all my weekends away and the various problems at work, I have not yet found the time to go visit her. I told you that my clinic has decided to open a branch in the city and then the doctor asked me to always do a few days in Matera to train the new secretaries. But those who were chosen are so stupid that if I tried to teach them even just how to answer the phone, they still would not be able to do it after an whole year. Now I started to interview other girls because even my boss finally realized that other then a pretty face, they don't have much to offer and it would be good to change them before they cause too much damage. Anyway, back to your mother. No news, I'm sorry."

"You know, even when I saw her tonight, it's weird but, I thought she felt uncomfortable around me. I think most older people are less able to accept the fact that almost all of their children are far away. You'll see that from now on she will impose those dinners on us more often. She does not understand that it is not easy for us to come back here. And anyway, she always has Amaia. I understand that it is different to have only one child close than having four, however, the life you have to build is where your work is, otherwise you end up just trying to survive."

"Did you ever think of coming back here to live?" Stella asked with a faint inflection of hope in her voice.

"I thought of leaving Milan, yes. It is nearly a decade that I've lived in that city, and I've begun to feel the need to change. And you know, I went to visit my siblings around the world and have a great desire to follow them. To travel more. But where could I live? I do not know. But back here? No way! You know that I have this type of allergy to small towns. I always feel as though all eyes are on me. All ready to watch your every step. And most of the time it's not just a feeling. I love this place. My best memories are here, and when I come here I always feel pampered and spoiled. It's like being a child again and again. But I know it's my weakness, prejudice, and the chatter of the people blocking me. I prefer to live in a place where you can feel free, light, albeit with a lot more responsibility. And now, I don't even think about it. I'm so close to becoming a junior partner in my law firm now that I would not think of changing for anyone or anything."

"I understand, although sometimes I think it would be really nice to have you back in my daily life."

"It would be nice, yes" and a slow sigh came out from her lips. A smile then took its place. "But you know! We made that promise years ago. We will spend our retirement together, anywhere you want" and other chatter and laughter and serenity of the old days came bursting back.

"So, tell me a bit about the search for a husband?" Selin laughed expecting Stella to laugh with her. But when she saw her lower her eyes and blushing slightly she began to jump in her chair and scream "whaaaaaaaaat? You have not said anything bitch" she teased her smiling, "do you really think you can avoid the question in a such elusive manner? If you don't tell me everything at once, you can forget me spending my retirement years with you. Spit it out!" In order to look intimidating, she raise her arm and pointed her index toward Stella's face.

"But what makes you think that I will hide something. Come on, there is nothing to say. Nothing important anyway."

"I love the unimportant things ... So?" And then she went into her stubborn silence "Oh man, you've totally lost your mind for this guy."

"But nooooo. It is the usual hobby of the weekend, it's nothing serious"

"Oh yes? So tell me how long is that you are hanging out with this particular hobby?"

"A bit more than three months," she said, laughing and screaming "I cannot believe it, I'm losing my mind."

"Yeeeeeeeesss" echoed Selin, happy for her best friend who was a step closer to achieving her dreams at last. "Does he have a name, or do I have to call this guy 'hobby' for the rest of my life?"

"Andrea. He works as a teacher in Matera. We met at work because one day he accompanied his niece for a visit to the doctor and asked me the phone number. That weekend we went out together and we laughed so much, I do not know how to explain it but it seemed like I knew him for so long. And we both like to do new things, try crazy things. Often he picks me up after work to have dinner or even just to say hello."

"Does it make you happy?"

"Yes," said Stella, with a sigh, her eyes lost in day dreaming. "When I'm with him I'm not afraid of anything. I feel like I am the queen of the world. I hope it lasts."

"My darling, you have had many adventures and in all these years I've never once seen you like this, not even remotely close to this. Whatever it is, it's special. This, I can say it with confidence" and abandoning her chair she dived into Stella's arms. "Okay, a toast to you and Andrea... may only the best happen to you." And she lifted the glass of wine up to meet hers. And they drank ... And again ... And drank... spoke at length, as if those eleven years of separation had never happened, as if they were still the two friends who lived just two blocks away. That they could still see each other every day after school, picturing a shining future for both of them.

CHAPTER III

Finally the Saturday night arrived and with it, the famous dinner that her mother had planned for some time. There was no occasion in particular on account of the evening. Only the pleasure of having all her children together in the same room and under the same roof.

The night before, she had been the first to go home and had just enough time to rest her head on the pillow but had fallen into such a deep sleep that she did not have time to chat with the sisters. That morning, she woke up quite early out of habit finding her mother already up and fully operational. Both the mother and her older sister were busy cooking some delicious dishes that would be part of the evening menu. Definitely a new invention of her mother, smelling very inviting and looking stylish. Her father had left home very early that morning to go to the countryside to take care of her beloved plants.

She had the impression that the two were whispering about something in particular that they did not want her to listen to because she saw them quickly change the subject as soon as they heard her take the last few steps. Selin continued to have the feeling that something strange was happening but maybe it was just her being paranoid. As she was about to have a quick breakfast, one by one her siblings woke up and joined her. Voices vibrant and full of life filled the house after years of timid and at times muffled conversations. Satisfying the will of their mother, the morning passed between family obligations, which consisted of a visit to various relatives. Unfortunately, have to visit relatives was part of a few various duties that their mother had planned for the weekend and no one dared to disagree: Saturday meant to visit uncles and paternal grandparents, the only one that was still alive! Their luck was that at least for Sunday their mother had not set any program, and then would be free to do what they wanted. The problem was not that there were bad relations with relatives, or discord of any kind, simply that those two days of freedom from daily obligations, which living in their big cities forced them to face, they preferred to pass them otherwise. Simply free to sleep without worries, eat huge amount of healthy food and spend as much time as possible with old friends.

But those were the agreements and given the determination of their mother, no one was willing to challenge them. Quickly spent the day within half an hour dedicated to an uncle and another dedicated to another, to pop by grandparents who invariably found them way too slim and tried to force them into eating as much as possible at any time, without containment. And they all felt free to comment "Hey Selin, is that really you? we did not expect to see you. But how many years have passed?" But she was not the only one to live out of town, thought Selin, yet everyone seemed to have only noticed her absence. Selin felt under observation and therefore uncomfortable for all the time they were visiting relatives. Probably that same sense of not belonging to that place, that had always accompanied her life, was visible for them. Fortunately a few hours later and the torture got to an end. In the afternoon the parents wanted to rest and went to lie down on the bed while the younger ones were looking for a way to keep themselves busy. Amaia began to prepare the fresh orange juice using the oranges that her father had brought home the day before from the countryside. She cut them in half, and only put the squeezed juice in a bottle and threw away the pulp. She said that her children loved it. Arianna was looking at her old schoolbooks and artworks that she remembered doing in the past. She wanted to look into them to formulate new ideas. Stefano, however, exchanged messages with his deputy to see if everything was al right in his bar. Selin took her place at the table, she stole a little bit of orange juice from her sister, because she basically was dying to try it and, turning to her two other siblings, she said, "how often do you come home?"

"Well I come back two, three times a year depends on ... Christmas and Easter time for sure and, if I can, a week in summer time" replied Arianna impetuously, drowned in books that now surrounded her as a precarious wall while she sat on the floor beginning to lose hope of being able to find what she was looking for, "but I remember that they were here!" she exclaimed to herself.

"I come back at Christmas for sure ... I arranged with my deputy to take Christmas off and he takes New Year. His family lives there and he still manages to get lunch in the family so it's in both interests. Easter I cannot always do, but in the summer I always try to arrange with Arianna to come back on the same weekend so we are together. So I definitely come back twice a year most of the time," her brother said.

"I do not understand. Me too! I always come back a couple of times a year and yet everyone tells that they are so surprised to see me?" said nervously Selin "This juice is really good," she added, turning to Amaia.

"Thank you my dear. But you do realize that you never come back twice a year but rather once every two years, right?" Replied the eldest.

"But no, it's not true!" Selin said annoyed.

"Please, see that Ama is right" Arianna emerged from behind the books to answer. "You come back home once every two years because so many times you say you'll come but then you cancel at the last minute. Then at Christmas you never come because you say that you do not like to travel in the holidays because it is too chaotic. You do come back sometimes over the summer holiday to get a bit of the Southern sea, and you never say anything to Stefano and I so that you can take care of your own business: go to the sea without being disturbed and go out with your friends in the evening."

"But Ari, you and me, we saw each other last summer and with Stefano too just a few months ago ... so it is not true that we don't see each other."

"And that's just because you came to visit us in Barcelona and London. But if your question is about this place, our home town, Bernalda, well no dear, you come back here as little as possible. For us it is not a problem because me and Arianna have no trouble to visit you in Milan or you travelling to our cities but you see our parents more or less once every two years and considering your intolerance to the relatives I would say that you don't see our uncles for centuries" concluded Stefano.

"Come have a little more juice"' said Amaia to stop the direction towards which the conversation was heading. Selin's facial expressions clearly told her that she was beginning to feel uncomfortable in her own shoes.

Selin accepted the juice not knowing what else to replicate. Her siblings were right, she had confused her travelling twice a year with her returning home twice a year. Which was not entirely true. When was the last time she had seen her aunt and uncle? And suddenly a thought struck her, "Amaia, but when was the last time we saw each other you and I?"

"Don't think about that, come on. You were busy at work. I understand. We are all here now and that's what counts."

Well, Amaia could say that it did not matter, but she realized that it was nearly four years that she had not seen her sister. The last time she came home now a couple of years before, she had spent the entire time at the seaside and had not even asked her to join her or go and visit her. She felt so ashamed of herself. A scream of joy coming from over her shoulders, told her that the youngest sister had finally found the book that she was looking for, interrupted her train of thought and broke that feeling of shame that was spreading in her body. Selin tried to convince herself that Amaia didn't seem to have taken this personally or cared at all. And she continued, now with a sense of greater relief, to sip the juice, asking "Can I help?"

It reached seven o'clock and with it the time to finally all sit at the table and share their lives in recent months. It was incredibly pleasant. She had forgotten how beautiful the family atmosphere was. All sitting around the big table in the living room with tasty and delicious dishes that filled every corner of the house and that alternated with others, if possible, even tastier. Mum had cooked all by herself with a little help from Amaia while the other siblings, less skilled in the kitchen, helped to set the table and began to pour the wine into the glasses. Yes, that they knew how to do. Everyone decided to dress particularly well to honour their mother. Amaia a simple outfit, black pants, a beige sweater and décolleté with a minimal heel; her brother had avoided the tie but otherwise looked ready to go to a wedding.

The blue shirt with thin stripes, trousers of dark shades made him a model and his sisters could not help admit that they had a really fascinating brother. Her little sister opted for a short but no vulgar dress as suggested by his youthful fresh face and curvy body. She never seemed vulgar. Everyone in her family had inherited the elegant and refined demeanour that allow them to wear anything without falling in the gross look. She had a strapless dress, tight at the top that became soft when it had to embrace her hips and her legs. It was black with bands of pink on the front. And over a black sweater, wide, transparent and long sleeves that left one shoulder free to cover it from the delicate spring coolness. And transparent stockings and high heels completed the whole outfit. For a bit of extra money on the side, her sister was a model for small-scale parades or for newspapers and magazines.

And finally Selin. She had opted for a black pencil skirt with a side slit and a soft red T-shirt that left both free shoulders and red high-heeled shoes. She had promised to her best friend to join her clubbing if dinner wasn't going to last hours and hours. Surely the appearance of young boys, independent, responsible and proud unleashed in her mother a gesture of pride that does not verbalize, but it was quite clear through her eyes.

Her mother began to entertain them with small town stories where they seemed to become vitally important events in their lives now seemed petty. But there was something fun about having to pretend that they were those incredible events, when true was there was absolutely nothing interesting about it. "Can you believe your cousin began dating that girl. But did you know that her family doesn't have a good reputation? It is said to have dangerous connections."

"Mum how can you not get tired" scolded laughing Arianna "still hear the rumours of those people that have to build up fake stories about others to make themselves more attractive?"

"Okay, okay. I stop it! Since my small town stories are not enough for you. Then you'll have to talk to us because I have nothing more to say. Who starts?"

"Me, I start." It was her brother's turn to share how his business was going and how it seemed difficult at times to face it all alone. Be his own boss had its cons. Whatever happened was his responsibility. Each problem had to be solved by him and also as quickly as possible. How many times he had to improvise as a painter, electrician, HR, chef, etc. How often dissolute bartenders left without warning, sometimes with a single message, and he always had to find an efficient solution with the speed of light.

Sometimes it was exhausting but the rewards that he was getting were so many that he could not feel more proud of himself and what he was doing. And even his parents were very proud. He told them about something happened only a few months before when a famous Spanish actor had entered to eat in his bar and the two had started chatting and laughing together. He did not know he was an actor who was considered a VIP in Spain. A few days later he reappeared with a group of collaborators and told him who he was and that he planned to record scenes of the film that he was producing in the bar. A month later he came back with the whole crew to film. "It was crazy, you cannot even begin to imagine. These huge lights placed everywhere, cameras at various angles, the director screaming all the time and a lot of actors. They were filming the scene in which a guy meets a girl clandestinely. She was a married   spy. So not only was she passing state secrets to him, but they were also having an affair. It was really exciting. The film should be released next year and they have promised to send me an invitation to the première and also to mention my bar in the credits. This guy still comes to my bar drinking and always brings many girls with him. He is now one of my loyal customers."

Then it was Arianna's turn to speak and she was difficult to contain. She spoke of all the magical and wonderful things that she discovered each day. Her life was like a book. An incredible tale of adventure and magic. Everything was so fabulous in her world. She told them of the latest fashion show she had participated in last month. It was for a showcase of wedding dresses in central London, and she had the opportunity to wear the most outrageous outfits that anyone could imagine: wedding dresses of red, green or pearl, some so short that no one would never even think of getting married in them, others with trains meters and meters long. The best part was to finally try, or rather devoured, all the wedding cakes she wanted immediately after the parade. "I had to be on a diet for a couple of weeks before that show and in an hour I was able to take back all the lost pounds. However, thanks to the show I got a bit of cash."

"Honey are you sure you still do not want me and your father to help you a bit with the expenses?" Asked the mother anxious.

"Mum, if I was broke, I would tell you. Believe me. Being poor does not suit me," Arianna said with irony. "These modelling gigs help me a lot and occasionally I can even sell some of my photographs. Oh, by the way I have created a website where the public can buy my photos. In this way, I have the opportunity to sell them worldwide. I started last year and I'm selling more and more and more photos and, you know, that last month I had to send one all the way to Hong Kong! How cool is that? Oh, and I did not tell you the last of it. A few weeks ago I began to also contact some art galleries to see if they would take some of my paintings or photographs and they have now managed to place two photographs in a photo exhibition where the theme is *details*. They chose two of my photos with an eye photographed close-up in which it seems there is a galaxy within it and the other of a raindrop barely touching the ground. But then two weeks ago I was contacted because they would like to have my paintings in a temporary exhibition of young emerging artists.

Do you understand guys, for six months some of my paintings are going to be arranged in a London gallery. Of course I will not be paid for this, but the paintings are still for sale, and at the end of the show someone might decide to buy them."

"Ari, I've always known that yours is a unique talent. Just promise me that if you ever get in any trouble you will let us know as soon as possible, okay?"
"Sure, Mum, for now the modelling job and selling photographs are enough for me. And then I have to bite the bullet for another year and finish my photography course and then at least I will not have to pay the school."
"And we all know that you can do it sister" interjected Amaia "It has always been clear in your mind what you want to do with your life and with a lot of grit and determination you're succeeding. Everyone can see that."
"You can say that again," replied her brother with conviction.
"And you Amaia what do you have to share with us?" Selin intervened to postpone the moment when she would be having to speak.
Everyone knew what was really special in the world of her sister, Amaia. In fact, his sister could talk for hours and hours without getting tired about her small treasures, her children. So much so that they had to find a way to change the subject to divert her mind from those little chubby dolls that were waiting for her only a few blocks away and she missed them as if they had been taken away by a stranger and did not know if she would ever see them again. "Last week Miki played his first football tournament between the schools of Basilicata and his team won. Mum and Dad came to watch the match, Miki

was good, right?" At the nodding of her parents head Amaia went on on talking

"And Jenny had her first crush."

"But she's only four?!?" cried her brother between amusement and horror.

"I know, I know, but this year she has started to show special care for this child which makes kindergarten together and that sometimes comes home to spend the afternoon when his working mother cannot find a babysitter. And you should see how Jenny gets angry when she notices that he is with the other friends and ignores her a bit. And when they are alone he does whatever she tells him to do. He is her slave."

"Eh, if I know the kind, I know that little Jenny will soon find herself heartbroken," her brother said in seriousness.

"Or maybe she's a really lucky girl and has already found the man of her life... or rather the child of her life," Arianna laughed heartily.

"My little Jenny. Okay, now I will stop talking or you will be forced to put up with stories about your grandchildren for the whole evening. By the way Selin, you're the only one that has not yet updated us on her life. What will you tell us?"

In listening to the stories of her siblings and parents, Selin began to feel lonely, empty, dull. As if all that focus on success, that desire for the important work she did, made her forget to observe the world around her. She tried to delay the moment when she had to talk about herself as much as possible because she felt she had nothing to say. Her eyes would not have lit up by telling her life story because every day she just woke up, went to fight in the courtroom with someone and came home, showered, watched movies and read. And the next day the same. She had created a wall around herself over the years that was increasingly difficult to overcome. Her house was empty. No one was waiting for her and no one was going to visit and have a chat. She had no children to come home to, she had no adventures that were waiting behind the door, and there were no challenges to face. Nothing at all! For a moment she tried to remember why she had chosen to live in a grey and cold city that she would never call home and why she chose to make a job in which she knew every secret and now acted so automatically that it stopped stimulating and intriguing her long ago. Had she become a cold robot?

Yet for some reason, these thoughts had never entered her mind until now. But somehow listening to her siblings having so many things that captivated and stimulated them, made her do a quick mental comparison of her existence. Oh my God! She didn't even have a hobby. She was not even in the gym or running or just walking in the park. What did she have besides work? And was there still something in her work that motivated her and made her feel excited? Unfortunately for her, the answer to those questions was a clear and simple no. Life was now just habit and a race for success. But it was enough for her that she had tried in life and achieved. It was enough! With a false and exaggerated enthusiasm she tried to share her life updates, emphasizing things so she could prolong her speech over the two simple words that it was worth spending.

"Well, the promotion should be just around the corner. Soon I will be the youngest partner in the firm and they will give me a bigger office, more money and more complex cases. Also, once I become a partner, will take part in amazing evening gala and charity events and I will take charge of the good name of my company. And I will also have the opportunity to wear long and very elegant dresses. About that Ari, I meant to ask you if you could create some stylish dresses for me so I can really be the only one to own and wear them. In my environment, be able to wear a high couture dress is a sign of power."

"Sure sister. Just tell me what you have in mind and I will do it," said Ari.

"My dear, it sound really interesting" said her mother.

Somehow she managed to fool everyone and to hide the emptiness she felt inside.

After a while her mother spoke again, and with a satisfied smile said, "My children, I am truly the luckiest mother in the world. You know how to make me proud."

Suddenly a sad light permeated through her eyes and began gently to hold her husband's hand in hers and after a deep breath began to speak again. "I know I was particularly pressing lately and I have insisted way too much to have all my children here with me tonight. Well, there was one thing I needed to share with you all that I didn't want to say on the phone. So I apologize for these months answering torture to which I have submitted you to, I realize that I really went over the top at times," she said looking at Selin.

"You should know that about a month ago I went to my doctor for a check-up. I just felt this continuous pressing in my stomach and a feeling of constant fatigue and did not understand why. I always did my morning walks and did not eat anything strange. Now since you left home we eat only products that your father takes us from the countryside. Everything really is natural! The doctor advised me to do a more thorough check up because at a first glimpse I had nothing. I'm sorry I have not said anything before but I didn't want to make you worry. I started doing a series of checks, one after another and eventually three weeks ago they have informed me of the outcome. I'm sorry to give you this news as well but my children, unfortunately postponing it no longer makes sense. Doctors have found that I have cancer."

After a few minutes of general dismay and silence, it began an increasingly loud buzz and questions about it. Questions began to hover in the air.

"Why did you not say anything? We would have come immediately …."

"What does the doctor thinks?"

"Do you have to get surgery?"

"Do you have to do chemio?"

"When is the next visit?"

"What kind of cancer do you have?"

"Do you still feel pain in the stomach?"

"Have you already begun treatment?"

"Which hospital are they treating you in?"

"How long will you have to follow the treatment?"

"How long does it takes to heal?"

The questions that followed numbered in the thousands and at some point began to merge into each other. They followed one another so quickly among the three siblings that the mother did not even have time to think clearly and process a response. The only one that did not utter a word was the older sister. Taking advantage of a quiet moment Selin spoke directly to her and raising the tone of her voice so that everyone could hear her, she began to ask, "You knew about this already, didn't you?"

The older sister did not dare to look at anyone in the eye nor to answer but simply remained where she was, motionless. The mother was speaking in her defence this time. "Amaia and your father are the only people to know about this. Your sister knows just because she had to drive me to all the appointments and was there when the doctor gave me the results. If she did not tell you anything guys, it's just because I asked her not to."

Suddenly, as if from a distant planet, her sister spoke in a voice so thin and pleading that resembled a frightened puppy more than a mature, independent, adult woman with an incredibly strong character. "Please mum, tell them the truth, tell them the rest," and her eyes were now filled with tears - her fists clenched so that the nails were sticking in the palm of her hand to keep her from bursting into tears.

"What is it mum? Anything else?" asked Arianna with big tears that began to fill her eyes.

"Okay, okay, the doctor also said something else. He said that I discovered my sickness too late, which means that it is at an advanced stage and that it is useless to do any treatments because it would not achieve anything and only weaken my body further. It will cause me physical suffering without getting concrete results. It might add at most a couple of months to my existence, but at the expense of quality. I would spend two months longer attached to a machine. The fact is, in the end, I have three to six months of my life left and that's why for the last time, I wanted to have my entire family back together under one roof, gathered around the same table even if only for a couple of days."

Her voice was now only a graceful breath and copious tears began to scratch her face holding back a few seconds between the wrinkles around the eyes before rushing rapids along her cheeks and relentlessly abandoning her body while her hands more intensely than ever wrapped themselves around those of her husband.

"I wanted to tell you guys that I love you so much and that I am absolutely satisfied with the life that I lived. I do not regret anything. I could not wish for anything more. I have got you all, and you're the best thing that anyone could wish for and I want you to know that although every now and then I am a bit too harsh, criticizing your choices, looking unhappy, I never intended to do so. You are all perfect just as you are. So perfect. And I could not love you any more".

While her hand continued to hold that of her husband to find the strength and support she needed, she found herself surrounded by the arms of her younger daughter wrapped around her neck with a sudden snap, getting up and dropping the chair thunderously. Arianna ran around the table and sobbed loudly throwing her arms around her mother's neck and tried to hold her as tight as her slender body allowed her. The older sister on the other hand remained in her place, in the same position as before with her head still looking down. Except that now it was not possible to further hold back the tears that ran down her face silently. Her brother, shining eyes, somehow showed the strength not to cry but left his seat to join the little sister in embracing their mother. The only thing he could say was a feeble "Mum", barely audible.

Selin did not know what to think. It was as if she observed the scene as a foreign spectator - as if she didn't belonged there. It was like watching a movie, sitting comfortably in her chair at the cinema. A movie tearjerker sure, but still a movie. Unreal. That's how it seemed. She felt that everything inside her was still, it was as if her heart had stopped. She had never felt so empty, unfeeling, emotionless. She felt only an icy grip tighten around her heart. She did not cry, did not react, barely noticed the breathing. Once again she had not realised what was happening within her own family. All that could not be real.

It was another horrific nightmare that had run over. And soon she would wake up covered in sweat, scared but with the knowledge that it was all fake. It was all fake. This reality was just a big lie. And she did not belong to it.

After a few minutes that seemed like an eternity in which the others continued to express their grief, she silently stood up and without a word, grabbed her purse from the chair behind her and slowly walked toward the stairs and so to the door slowly closed behind her. Like a distant noise she heard the mother whom with suffocated voice saying her name. "Selin ... stay, please." But she ignored it, ignored it all. She just wanted to walk and walk and so she did.

CHAPTER IV

She walked along like an automaton. Her blank stare ignoring those who recognized her in the street and tried in vain to attract her attention. She arrived at the border of the town, passed it and began to penetrate the arched streets of the countryside. The darkness of the night was not dark enough for her and the faint light that still persisted hurt her eyes. She could not remember how long she was walking for, nor where she was precisely at that moment because that feeling of infinite nothingness continued to wrap her tight. Her mind did not want to think, did not want to know. Every thought that tried to emerge shot back to the bottom of the abyss of her soul. She could not, really not, accept the harsh reality into which her mother had suddenly thrown her. It was a truth that she refused to accept.

It was just a bad dream from which it was hard to wake up, yet she knew that sooner or later she would wake up. She just needed a bit of time. Everything was fine, everything was normal.

Suddenly her eyes stopped seeing: a blinding light, getting closer and closer forced her to shut her eyes but she was not frightened. The void that invaded urged her to accept the inevitability of everything that happened around her.

"Hey, al right beauty? Do you need a ride somewhere?"

A young and cheerful voice crept into her mind, struck somehow her hearing and made its way into Selin's soul. She opened her eyes and realized that the blinding light belonged to a car that had approached close by in the meantime and that voice, belonged to a young boy, certainly much younger than her. Carefree and cheerful with eyes full of light and vitality which, much to her surprise, Selin envied with her whole being. Two other friends were with him in the car. All happy, all cheerful, all alive. Suddenly she felt she had to do something to feel alive again, to steal even a minute of that overwhelming light-heartedness from these guys. She wanted to be in their company a little more. She did not want to get caught again by that incredibly dark night. The loneliness threatened to take her to thoughts that she was not yet ready to face. She wanted to run, be crazy, be immersed in life.

Suddenly, before she even became aware of it, she heard a woman's voice, numb and far away, which made it difficult to recognize as her own, asking: "Where are you guys going?"

The driver, who was obviously the group's leader, told her that they were going to Matera, to their usual pub. A really cool place with live rock music where one could dance until dawn and the drinks were cheap.

"It's such a cool place," the boy repeated. The way he spoke convinced her conclusively that these guys could not have been more than twenty-two or twenty-three years old, but that joy in her voice was a safe anchor for her.

"Do you have one more space for me?" she found herself asking. But who was that girl totally devoid of a sense of responsibility, who chatted with the guys whom she just met as if they were old friends? And even proposed to take a ride in the car together. Get in a car with strangers? She had never done that, especially not as her own suggestion! Not that it didn't happened in the past. Boys had approached her and offered a "spin", but she had always had enough brains to run away at the speed of light and return to public places where no one could hurt her.

Even her irresponsible and reckless best friend, Stella, would not have been so completely thoughtless. But when she heard the boy yell, "Hey buddies, make some space for her!" she realized that that night her life no longer belonged to her. Her well-defined road was about to suffer an irreparable shock. Her prudence, her foresight, somehow had abandoned her and without even a moment's hesitation, she climbed into the car and before she knew it had started drinking beer which magically appeared from under the seat of these strangers, much younger than her, who were preparing to drive her somewhere.

Twenty minutes later, Selin found herself in this pub with music so loud that she could not even hear her own thoughts. And the band, rather than singing, sounded like they had someone tightening a rope around their throats. The other two passengers of the car, whose names she had found to be Luca and Fabrizio, had gone to get more alcohol at the bar and it looked like it would take a while because the place was completely packed. Davide the driver, however, proclaimed himself as guide of the place and walked her around the entire place that was bigger than she had imagined at first, and above all very full of people. So much so that it was hard to breathe. She discovered that this place was really famous in the surrounding area. She found herself wondering if her friend Stella knew it. Thankfully they moved away from the crowd who danced, jumped and shook their head frantically to the rhythm of the so-called music to move to another room full of chairs and armchairs and various types of games and, most importantly, an amount of people that was bearable. There were several pool tables, darts and other games whose names she did not know. There was, for example, a table with a small disc that player try to fit into a tiny hole on either side of the table. Of course, there were football related games. She never understood why people would show so much interest in those classic pub games which she had always considered the pastime of drunks.

She admitted that she never had a great social life and that her idea of fun was to drink a glass of rosé wine whenever she successfully concluded a legal dispute at work. But really, she did not understand what drove people to waste their evenings getting drunk, hopping to the beat of rock and roll 'music' and throwing a few balls into holes. But shutting her thoughts down, putting her usual self aside, she realized that that night nothing was usual and, with the help of the beer that Luca and Fabrizio brought in the meantime, the loud music began to contact a part of herself which she never knew existed. She began to play, she began to relax, she played pool for the first time in her life with monstrous results. But she was amused. It surprised her even to laugh, to laugh out loud and talking about anything like a teenager playing with guys who had just left the age of adolescence. After two hours, her mind felt so lighter than it had ever been before, like there were no problems at all. Everything was fine.

Forgetting how many beers she had drunk by the time the two boys had already been gone for a while because, by their own admission, they needed to explore the area and hunt some nice chicks. Selin found those guys so adorable and tender that she really hoped they were going to find someone for the evening. She began to realise that she had always misjudged young guys.

She had never realised that they had that incredible and moving sweetness and that tender, and a little clumsy, behaviour that could win anyone over; in a certain way they deserved to win over anyone. Who knows why she always had this kind of prejudice against those who were younger than her. She actually realised that she had simply misjudged all those who were open to life, who were prepared to take risks. Perhaps because she was so terrified that she could never allow herself to take such risks herself. And so, she spent her entire life hiding in the most incredibly predictable routine. The fact that she did not know where the boys were gone for the past couple of hours, gave her hope that everything was going well for them. She stayed with Davide.

"I am sorry that the guys have abandoned us. I hope you don't take it personally but you know, we guys like to hunt when we go in pubs," Davide said.

"Actually, your friends are way too nice and I feel like I have just become their biggest supporter. If there is anything I can do to make them easier to hunt, let me know," said Selin sipping her beer, now a little tipsy. "The only thing I'm really sorry about it is that you seem to be stuck here with me. Your friends were smart enough to get away first. With me next to you, your hunt will be compromised."

"Don't worry about it. Actually, right now I'm selecting my prey." And pretending to fix invisible glasses with his right hand, he winked at her and stared at her from head to toe and back up again.

Bursting into a loud laugh Selin said, "I guess you must be really unlucky my friend... this meat has gone bad a long time ago. Compared to you I am an old woman. You could very nearly be my son."

"But I'm not, right?"

"Right," she agreed, "But I'm sure you can find better. You just tell me who you like and I will procure it to you on a silver plate." It was his turn now to laugh.

"Do not laugh, I'm serious. And if you want to know the truth, I am not all that great between the sheets," she said winking.

"Then I'll make sure there are no sheets in the proximity. Is that better?"

"What I'm saying is... I want another beer and then I want to find out what's in that room," said Selin pointing in the direction of a door that had not yet being explored.

"Oh, let's go grab a beer and then I'll show you the mysterious room," he said.

The mysterious room turned out to be a small room with other games, especially video games. In fact, the age of the boys in there was around eighteen or so. They decided to return to the previous room.

The more time they spent together, the more Davide turned out to be one of the most open and genuinely nice guys she had ever met. And patient too! He had had to explain all the rules of all the games they played and had not walked off when they played pool and a ball jumped off the table and hit him in the chest, or when she dropped his mug of beer resting on the corner of the pool table. And she could not even pay him back because she had left her wallet at home and in the rush to escape had forgotten to grab it and put it in the purse with all the other staff. So not only did he pay for her drinks the whole evening, but he also had to pay twice for himself. She felt so mortified but she could not help it. And, admittedly, he had been good at not make her feel guilty. Although at some point in the evening she thought he would lose his cool when they were playing darts and one would definitely have stabbed his arm if he did not have the reflexes to move so quickly. Fortunately, he loved to joke about everything.

However, the near miss hinted that it was better for her and for the people around her if she stopped playing and so, innocently, she looked Davide in the eye and said "let's go dancing." She thought that at least she could not do too much damage dancing. They laid the cues on the table, to the relief of Selin, and moved in the other room where they were immediately overwhelmed by the deafening music and reached the centre of the room where they began to move their bodies trying to imitate a harmony that the music could not properly communicate. Near them, Fabrizio was also on the dance floor with a girl possibly under age, or just become such, completely devoted to the rock style as suggested by her looks, with dark tones and piercings everywhere. Fabrizio, with his naively enthusiastic and happy attitude to have found a girl to keep him company for the evening, came to quickly update us that Luca had also succeeded in his mission and left the room for almost an hour with a girl who lived nearby. And after an enthusiastic 'high five' with Selin and David, Fabrizio returned to entertain his conquest. Unfortunately, after only a few minutes Selin noticed that as they danced, she happened to crush his foot - over and over again. Her awkwardness was following her everywhere that night. But Davide pretended not to notice and Selin was eternally grateful for that. After she and Davide danced for a while like irresponsible kids who had nothing to lose, he pulled her close, placed his lips close to her ear to be heard over the loud music and asked: "Are you having fun?"

It was probably because of alcohol or perhaps the thumping music which drowns her own thoughts, or perhaps the smile that the boy continuously had printed on his face that she said "yes". Yes, she was very much enjoying every bit of the night. But at that moment she decided that she did not want to just tell him with words, she wanted to prove it and wanted to somehow thank him. She began to think that the boy deserved to be lucky that night.

Thus, she stopped dancing, wrapped her arms around his neck and moved her face closer to his, placed her lips onto his and gently separated them until it became more decisive and move at a pace that was uniquely theirs. They continued kissing extensively and for a long time, totally oblivious to the world around them. Selin could feel the desire growing more and more inside Davide, his greedy lips and his curious hands wanted to learn more about her body. She felt his hands move further and further down, stroking her back and then further down towards the buttock where his hands lingered in long exploration. After what seemed like an eternity, they finally emerged from that kiss, dilated pupils, accelerated breathing and an irrepressible desire to have more. It wasn't a surprise to hear Davide say the words "Let's get out of here." The real surprise was to hear herself say, "Yes!" before she even have time to think.

She had never had a one-night stand, just as she had never been with younger boys; just as she had never entered into a disreputable pub or into any pub with strangers. But here she was, nearly thirty years old, doing this without stopping to think whether it was right or wrong, without thinking about the potential remorse the next day. She did not even care whether there would be a tomorrow or not. She just needed to feel alive now, that night, to feel that her heart was still beating. Davide grabbed her hand and making space between the crowd, dragged her out of there. Closing the door behind themselves, she was immediately struck by the silence of the night.

"Who knows what time it is?!" wondered Selin. They were all inside enjoying the night. Around them, only a few people in need of nicotine, or something else. She was not exactly an expert in the field. And above all, her mind was quickly attracted to something different. Strange movements inside the cars. In most cars. Bodies moving. Oh my God! But, but, but ... impossible! People were having sex in the car, in front of the pub where everyone could see them. But did they feel no embarrassment? Suddenly, she wondered if she was about to do the same. After all, she did not have a home there, and she certainly could not take him to her parents' house. And he was only twenty-three years old so probably still living with his mother.

Suddenly she regretted not asking more question about him and his life. She was surprised to emit a sigh of relief when Davide started up his car and came out of that parking lot. However, Selin could not now restrain herself from asking, "where are we going?"

"Me and some friends rented a garage just outside the town to rehearse for our band so to speak in a very amateur way during the week. I play the guitar, Fabrizio the drums, Luca sings and then there are another couple of our friends who help us. But at the weekend we all go to pubs so no one uses the garage. It will all be for us."

"And how will your friends go back home?" asked Selin seized with a sudden moment of clarity.

"Don't worry, we are warriors," said he smiling "They'll find a way."

She liked this guy. She liked his spontaneity, his freshness in speaking, the self-confidence, as if nothing bad could ever happen to him and to those who were in his company. It amused her to think that under normal circumstances, she would not even consider a guy like that! She would have considered him way beneath her possibility, as if only few guys could be considered at her 'level'.

After a quarter of an hour spent chatting about this and that, here they were, back in their small town, in their Bernalda. Davide parked the car in a small dimly lit street. It was the oldest part of the country. She had probably been there a few times as a teenager girl but it must have been more than a decade that she did not step foot in there. She recalled that this was the area where during the summer the kids would gather to play ball or hide and seek or something like that because there were few inhabited houses so no one complained if made noise. It was probably still the same and this was the reason why they chose to rent the garage there. They could try all day until late and no one would complain. He got out of the car, Davide opened the gate of the garage right next to where they had parked.

Well, thinking about it, the place was definitely rustic. With all those musical instruments scattered around the room and jackets left there too, not to mention empty packs of chips thrown on the floor next to empty beer bottles and plastic bags. In one corner, a small table full of papers, probably scores from which they practised, in another corner a small refrigerator and along the wall next to the coffee table a two-seater sofa, brown, full of scratches that had probably been recovered from somewhere. Besides this, various posters of various group. And this was all the furniture of the room.

Taken by curiosity Selin approached the table and began to take a look at those loose papers. They were not just musical scores but also lyrics of songs that were not in any famous song she could recall.

"Have you written these songs?" asked curiously Selin.

"Mostly I play covers with my friends, but we're trying to write something ourselves. We have already knocked out a couple of songs but something is missing. Honestly, the music we make is decent but does not rock."

"Will you let me hear something one of these days?" Selin said, well aware that there would never be 'one of these days' because after that night she would probably have no desire to see him. Honestly, she could not imagine being in a normal adult relationship with that boy. The only reason she was there that night was... not to think!

"You should come to hear us play. We practise here practically every night. So you can tell me what you think. Well, of course we're not a band of professionals so you shouldn't have high expectations." And with that answer Davide reached out to touch her waist and gently pulled her to himself. And lowering the tone of his voice, he brought her face close to his and soon their lips touched in an almost shy awkward kiss which became more and more confident, intense and penetrating. Selin could feel the warmth of Davide's tongue inside her mouth and the desire of her growing bit by bit. His hand investigating with desire her back, her bum and her hips. Selin slid her hands under his T-shirt and slowly began to stroke his chest, slipping towards the waist and then coming back again to explore his warm and perfect chest. And then, sinking back with her hands down where she grabbed the edges of his T-shirt, she lifted it up beyond his head and threw it on the floor without being pretentious.

And there he was, a young and perfect body beneath her clumsy hands. For his part, Davide slid a strap of her dress and, as he kissed and caressed her shoulder, his other hand also slipped the other shoulder strap and in a short bit her entire dress was on the floor. His hand on her breast, his lips on her neck! Davide slipped a hand on her back and quickly released her from the heavy presence of the bra and did not have to wait long before her panties disappeared soon after from her body. He even frantically freed himself of his jeans and boxers and between frantic kisses and exploring hands, he pushed her to the couch where he laid her down and where Selin could feel the male weight of his body on her. Davide leaned up to the height of her breast and began greedily licking a nipple and bite it as his hand massaged the other. Meanwhile, Selin let himself be swept away by this sweet torture as she felt his hand leave her breast stroke her abdomen and further down where he began to fondle her in her most intimate areas. Selin felt forgotten emotions that she had not felt for a long time overwhelming her.

Was it possible that in recent times she had simply excluded sex from her life? How can someone forget its beauty and intensity? She somehow felt she had to repay for this gift he was giving, which was to bring back her senses to life. She lifted his head from her breast and pushed his hand away from her clitoris... a part of her was already regretting it. She made him lie down on the couch, sat on him, bent down to kiss the mighty chest to begin with, and increasingly moving further down until hear him moaning.

Now it was his turn to feel tortured. Her tongue began to create gentle circles down the length of his body. And when her tongue touched the peak of his pleasure, she opened her mouth and welcome him inside. She wanted him to know, to feel, how much she was enjoying that very moment. And she continued to move her lips until she felt that he was about to lose control. She pushed her face from his most intimate part to give little kisses on his chest and face next to him said, "I want you inside me" and so they did. Grabbing his penis inserted it slowly inside her, deep and pervaded by an overwhelming passion began to move her body on top of him with increasing frenzy. The groans of both created a melody that echoed through the room. It was a wonderful torture that pervaded every centimetre of her body and that she would gladly continue indefinitely when suddenly her body went to meet a wonderful explosion of feelings that left her stunned, powerless but pleasantly satisfied.

She slid in beside him, putting her hand on his chest and serene slipped into a deep but short sleep, devoid of dreams or thoughts. A few hours of absolute nothing.

CHAPTER V

Still lying, one on top of the other, Davide fell asleep within a few seconds. His sleep revealed that angelic and naive features characteristic of his age. Selin soon felt lost with him in that restful sleep. It was only a few hours, and her eyes widened suddenly to a new reality. Her hand still resting on his chest, their legs still crossed and their nakedness inviolable evidence of the night before. She felt overwhelmed. She realized that the time was right to leave and put an end to such an intense night. She got up and quickly got dressed, being careful not to wake him. She wondered if she should leave a message. Usually in the movies the girls who run away always leave a note. But what could she write? Maybe a thank you for having paid for her beers all evening. Or maybe her phone number with a message to call. But she did not want to be called. Okay, they had fun, but the last thing she needed right now was a further complication. Maybe she could write something sensual and fun, like a thank you for making her come as a double-entendre to make him smile.

She grabbed pen and paper and her eyes fell again on the naked masculine body lying so close to her own naked feminine one. The serenity of that moment, the serenity of his face, was imprinted in her mind and she became aware of how any kind of closeness between the two of them would have only polluted that innocence. She was not serene, she was not happy, she was not the easy woman of a one-night stand that she claimed to be and she was not going to impose her heavy presence any further. The memory of the previous night was the most beautiful message that she could leave.

She grabbed her purse and walked out after a last fleeting and nostalgic gaze. Deeply nostalgic! as that night had made her turn away from an uncomfortable reality that she did not want to face. The cool night air finally woke her. She didn't know what to do, didn't know where to go. She began to search for the cell phone in her purse to see what time it was and if she could disturb her old friend Stella. The phone told her that it was almost five in the morning and also that during the night she had received dozens of calls from all her siblings and even her best friend. The music in the pub had probably drowned out the ringing, or perhaps it was her mind that refused to re-emerge into reality. Especially because some calls were only a few minutes earlier while she was wrapped in silence. However, she realised that among them there were many from Stella. She realized then that she was still awake and she could go to her house to rest. She was not ready to return to her family and look into her mother eyes and accept the inevitable. Chills pervaded her body but she could not determine whether it was because of her thoughts or the cold of the night.

Arriving in front of her friend's house, she rang the bell hoping with all her heart not to wake anyone up. Fortunately, Stella opened the door right after she rang, without even asking who was there, meaning that, yes, Stella was waiting for her. She threw her arms around Selin's neck and held it tightly. Her eyes red and swollen as if she had cried a lot that night. Selin let herself be wrapped by her friend's warm embrace without saying a word, knowing that she was in friendly arms.
She whispered in her ear, "where have you been? We were all so worried about you! Your sister called in distress and told me everything. I'm so sorry; I never imagined …" and heard her cry, probably not for the first time that night. Selin could not talk, not answer any of those questions. Stella walked away from her, grabbed her shoulders and between tears talked again "are you all right? You're so pale! Come on, here it's cold outside and you're only wearing this dress - you must be freezing! Come inside. A nice fire awaits us."

Wrapping one arm around her shoulder, Stella pushed her gently toward the inside of the house, up the stairs without a word, and helped her sit down in a chair nearby the fireplace. Stella sat down right in front of her. Selin, her hands resting on her thighs, one on top of the other, as to give herself some kind of self comfort. For the first time that night began to cry silent tears that bathed her cheeks and then one after another left her face. And then, with a sound barely audible, whispered "I'm sorry, I didn't want to worry you," Stella left her chair in a heartbeat to wrap her arms around her dear friend again. This gesture brought down the last of Selin's defences whom now burst into tears, deep and not stifled.

She continued to cry for a long time, shedding tears filled with a deep pain detained overnight. She wrapped herself in her friend's arms who could not do anything but make her feel her presence. For she knew she would never be able to find the right words to give her a little comfort, to give support to her best friend with whom as a child she had been fortunate to share many things, from the silly to the most intense. But she never wanted to share this moment with her. She knew that, even though her mother upset her many times she really loved her. In fact everyone loved Selin's mother. Over the years she had known how to respect and to love her incredible generosity and honesty. And the unconditional love she had always shown for her children. Suffering at seeing them walking away one after another, but proud of the future that they had been able to build with their own strength. Heck, she was not in any way tied to Selin mother but she felt lost when her older sister had called her on her cell phone the night before. She had hoped to find Selin with her and asked her to get in touch when Selin would show up -that's why Amaia called Stella. And when she revile her the 'news' of the day was deep the shock in Stella's face. Stella could still clearly remember the phone call. It was past ten o'clock and she was sitting comfortably on the sofa, in the arms of Andrea enjoying a movie on television and the warmth of the house when the constant ringing of the phone interrupted them. Answering the phone she heard the voice of Amaia. It had seemed odd since they had never had any kind of relationship and above all she had always felt judged by Amaia in her lifestyle.

"Hello Stella, I'm sorry to bother you so late. I just wanted to know if Selin was there with you."

"Don't worry, no bother at all, but I don't have any news of Selin since this morning," said Stella. And with a sense of agitation, she asked "didn't you have a family dinner tonight?"

"Er, yes, yes! Sure, we had dinner together." But that hesitant voice made her worry even more.

"Has something happened to Selin?" said Stella "you must tell me. She came from Milan for the sole purpose of participating in this dinner and I cannot believe she's gone, just out of the blue. And why would you need to look for her? She would say where she was going!"

"Please, could you just go home and check if she is nearby?"

"Yes, of course I'll be there in a few minutes." She did not know what was going on but had started to be seriously concerned "You must tell me what's going on."

Her sister took a deep breath and her voice trembled as she began to speak. Meanwhile her friend grabbed her purse and jacket and headed toward the car.

"I'm sorry to involve you. The truth is that our mother is not doing too well and when she told everyone tonight, well, Selin did not take it too well and she ran away. And now we have no idea where she might have gone. We are tremendously worried because she was completely in shock and honestly, I'm afraid that she would do something stupid; you're her best friend, so I though... I hoped, with my whole being that she came to you." She stopped talking and Stella sensed that she was trying not to cry.

"I haven't received any call from Selin but soon I'll be home and I'll be able to tell you if she's there. My parents are at home so if she came by they will tell me." And after a short pause of hesitation for fear of discovering something that she would not like, she took courage and asked, "What happened to your mother?"

And without further delay, she said "she has cancer... and only has about three months left to live".

Stella stopped suddenly in the middle of the road as she came close to the car and it seemed like the world around her had stopped. She could not speak, nor even think of anything to say. Not one thought crossed her mind. She remained motionless and silent for what had seemed like an eternity. It was Amaia's voice that called her back to reality "Stella, are you still there?"

Deeply shocked, she said "I'll call you when I get home." She hastily put the phone in her bag, grabbed the car keys and sped off.

She hoped with all her being that Selin was really at her house. Hopefully she rang the bell, her parents accommodated her and she stayed in their apartment. But why had she not tried to call her? Why had she not sought her help immediately? Her comfort? As she drove, she grabbed her cell phone from the purse with the sole purpose of reaching out to her childhood friend. All she heard was the phone ringing and ringing and ringing ... no answer. She decided to wait, and hope for better news once at home.

It was a bitter surprise when she realized that her house was surrounded by complete silence. She also went to wake her parents hoping they would be able to say something. But they knew nothing. She tried once again to call on her cell phone and still… no answer. She had to accept the fact that she didn't have the faintest idea where her closest friend in the world, one of the people whom she loved the most, who was going through one of the toughest moments of her life, was. She called Selin's sister and unfortunately had to tell her that she had no news but that she would continue to look for her and that she would immediately call her back as soon as she had any news. She spent the night calling Selin constantly, and at times she stood in the middle of the room taken by stupid thoughts like: who would prepare those fantastic cakes or sweets of all kinds? Or, but why had she not visited Selin's mother at all in the past few months? Perhaps in some way I could have helped her. Stella felt so overwhelmed by emotion that at some point she began to clean the whole house: she needed to keep herself busy and to avoid over thinking.

What a relief when, almost at dawn, she heard the intercom ring. She rushed down the stairs and was delighted to throw her arms around her friend's neck: happy to see her safe and sound, right there in front of her.

When Selin finally stopped crying, she could see the deep pain on her face accompanied by an incredible pallor. Gently she lifted Selin up from the chair and led her into the bedroom where she laid her down on the bed, gently placed a blanket on her body and stroked her hair gently, whispering, "Try to rest. Everything will be fine."

Selin did not speak, did not react. She simply let the silent tears streaming down her face. She closed her eyes and fell into a deep and dreamless sleep. Stella took advantage of the pause to call Amaia again and finally tell her that Selin was safe at her house and that she was now resting. Even over the phone, Stella could hear the sigh of relief that came from the other side of the phone.

"Oh thank you, thank you. We were so worried. No one was able to sleep tonight."

"Is it okay with you if I let her sleep and rest here? And then, when she feels better I will bring her back home."

"Of course, absolutely. The important thing is that she is well and... please just, once she wakes, tell her that we love her and that we wait for her to come back home."

"It will be done. See you soon."

Ending the call, she felt all the exhaustion of that overwhelmingly busy night and decided to try to catch herself a few hours of sleep too. And so she did. She lay down next to Selin, so that she would be found at her side if she woke up before her and she needed anything.

When she opened her eyes, she found Selin right in front of her staring at her with big, red and swollen eyes from crying. The image that she created in Stella's mind was that of a little and fearful child feeling lost, not knowing where to go and how to find the way back home.

"What now?"

"I don't know, honey. I don't know."

"But... it's my mum! I cannot lose her, how I can be without her?"

All that Stella could do was to stroke her hair and try to make her feel her support. She did not know what to say. She felt that all she could say to her simply did not make sense and seemed stupid, a cliché that it would be of no comfort at that time.

"I would go talk to the doctor" Selin said "Perhaps they did not understand what the doctor was actually saying. Maybe they heard the word cancer and thought the worst but, but today it is treatable. I mean, I think that something can be done. She has given up too quickly. I'm sure if I talk with the doctors, they will tell me that there are a lot of things we can still do. It will be the first thing I'll do tomorrow morning as the GP's surgery opens. Do you want to come with me?"

"Of course dear," she felt her heart clench in pain at seeing a dear friend so desperately clinging to an imaginary hope. "Do you want to eat something?" she asked, hoping to distract her somehow.

"No, I'm not hungry. But can I use your computer? I would like to do some research on the internet just to be prepared and understand what the doctor will tell me and maybe I'll also find information on some experimental treatment that my mum could try. And I could also try to find a hospital specializing in treating tumours where I could take my mother for further consultation."

"Of course, feel free to use my PC. It is in the living room. But Selin, your family is waiting for you. You should also think about returning to them and just being with them."

"Yes sure, sure... but first I have to do some research." And with that, she abandoned the bed and head for the living room where Stella heard her start the computer and compulsively press various buttons.

Meanwhile she sat on the bed trying to figure out what to do, how to help her friend and bring her back in some way to reality. She was clearly in shock and she was beginning to feel utterly powerless. She decided to go to the kitchen and prepare something to eat anyway in the hope that if she had found the food ready and under her nose, Selin would maybe stretched out her hand and ate something. She made small sandwiches and salad and put everything on the table where Selin was fiddling with the computer. She sat down and began to question her, hoping to distract her somehow.

"So tell me where you were last night? We all tried to call you a thousand times! We were very worried about you."

"Oh, you're right. I found the calls. I'm sorry, I didn't want to worry anyone. I was in a pub, there was loud music and I didn't hear the calls."

"You were in a pub?" She asked in surprise especially as Selin's voice was calm and indifferent as if it were totally normal for her to go to pubs. Especially after receiving the news that your mother is going to die. She would have expected it from herself but not from Selin. "What pub?"

"I don't know, but it was not here in the village. We went with the car to Matera and I honestly did not notice the name."

"We? You and who Seli?" Her voice alarmed.

"It doesn't matter. Really. Now I need to concentrate on my research if you don't mind. Oh damn! I almost forgot. I have to call my boss and tell him I'm taking a few days off from work. I'm discovering many optional treatments on the internet, so I'll probably have to talk to many doctors about them in the coming days. I cannot return to Milan now."

And with that she left the table and went to get her phone out of her purse to contact her boss, telling him that some circumstances that require her presence in town with her family had emerged, hoping that it will take only a few days at most. She closed the conversation and looked back at the computer screen, making notes on a piece of paper to her right whenever she found something she considered interesting.

She found a very curious study, further elaborated in recent years, for which the manifestation of certain diseases would be expressly correlated with the suppression of emotions. This study claimed that unexpressed emotions, especially anger and grief, were the cause of cancer related diseases. Apparently, the expression of emotions would always be tied to a specific flow of peptides in our body, whereby the chronic suppression of those, would results in a massive disruption of the psychosomatic network. According to this study, each of us has a number of small tumour cells which constantly grow. The part of the immune system responsible for the destruction of these errant cells consists of natural killer cells whose job is to attack these cells, destroying them to rid the body of every cancerous growth. In most of us, most of the time, these cells do their job properly, a job coordinated by various brain and body's peptides and their receptors, and these small tumours never grow large enough to make a human sick. But what if the peptides flow is interrupted? Is there a way to intervene consciously to ensure that our natural killer cells continue to do their job? Is emotional health somewhat connected with physical health? This school of thought considers all emotions to be positive because emotions are what unites the mind with the body. Anger, fear and sadness, the so-called negative emotions are healthy in the same way as peace, joy and courage. Suppressing those emotions, not making them flow freely, will cause it to act as a multi purpose rather than a unified whole. The stress that this causes, creates blockage and an insufficient flow of peptides at a cellular level: this is what triggers the conditions of weakness which can lead to diseases. Many psychologist also interpret depression as suppressed anger. But her mother had never seemed depressed, but had to admit she did not return in Bernalda that often and on the phone she was always trying to reduce the conversations to a minimum so, what did she know about her own mother? It marked a note on a block to remember to ask Amaia if their mother had recently shown signs of depression or, conversely, excessive anger. Selin continued reading and discovered that consequently, the ability to express these emotions in an appropriate manner, according to that study, should increase the chances of survival of patients. The site offered several alternatives for doing so, and the most efficient way consisted of a combo of various therapies, all based on cognitive-behavioural psychology: individual sessions, group sessions, outdoor activities and scream therapy. The latter was something she had never heard of but it seemed really interesting: a group of people, posed in various contexts who used the scream as a conduit to let their emotions go free.

Selin pointed scream therapy on her clipboard pad to be investigated in more detail later.

Meanwhile she began to read on another site that had also caught her attention and that she had left on the sidelines. That site claimed that our health was closely related to the food we eat. Certain types of foods are more likely to cause disease. In particular the casein in the milk, together with excessive consumption of meat, would increase the chance of diseases such as cancer, diabetes and heart attack. The higher the consumption of these foods, the higher the probability of developing a disease. However, it seemed to have been proved that it was possible to see an opposite effect. Reducing the consumption of milk and increasing the consumption of fruits, vegetables, legumes and grains may lead to an improvement for patients that have started to show the first symptoms. Well, her mother had always consumed a lot of dairy from what she remembered. So she added a note on the side of her notepad to eliminate dairy products from her mother's diet.

She felt overwhelmed by her research, she was learning so many new terms and concepts on how our body mechanisms' work. She found, for example, that cancer cells are called macrophages and she was not even sure if she had ever heard that word before in her life. She discovered that there was a theory that supported the use of growth hormones since adult macrophages do not replicate. As a result, growth hormones would cause the immature macrophage to grow and stop dividing.

So the rest of the day went by and Selin showed no sign of will to return home. Stella, meanwhile was receiving calls from Selin's sister asking when she was going back home. But she had no answer to this question, because every time she alluded to the idea of re-embracing her family, Selin answered, "I'm too busy doing research now, I cannot interrupt my work." And she was given the same answer even when she asked her just to talk on the phone with Amaia.

She did not eat anything all day! Stella tried again and again to pass food in front of the computer screen, but it was promptly put aside without being touched. She had also cut slices of apples desperately asking her to taste at least one, but it was like talking to a wall. She was so lost in herself, so busy looking for answers she could not pick up anything from the surrounding world and the only way she could convince her to go to sleep, when it was already two in the morning, was that in the morning she had to wake up early to meet the family doctor.

When she opened her eyes at seven in the morning she realized that Selin had been already awake for more than an hour, had already showered, changed into borrowed clothes from her closet - luckily they wore the same size - and she was once again typing on the computer keyboard because, "I'm still lacking some information." She went into the kitchen and made breakfast once again placed it on the table next to the computer hoping that she would spontaneously touch the food. And when she, while consuming her own breakfast, realized that Selin was not going to touch any food, with a firm voice, she ordered her to eat because if the doctor saw her so pale he would only ask questions about Selin's health and would have refused to explain anything about what was happening to her mother. She felt wicked treating her that way, as if she had to deal with a small and capricious child but somehow this was the only way to keep her healthy. Selin seemed to have lost her survival instinct, forgotten her primordial needs. She was completely immersed in its obsession to save her mother. At least this way she obtained the result of her eating a couple of biscuits. It was not much, but it was something.

After an hour they were with the family doctor trying to shed light on what her mother had exactly and what her options were. Unfortunately, the news they got was not what she expected. Her mother was in the last stage of breast cancer with no possibility of regression. Unfortunately, the tumour was there for some time but had gone unnoticed for a long time before it decided to show symptoms that her mother had neglected, taking them to be normal aches and pains, eye-strain, advancing age, etc. Two months earlier, her sister forced her mother, against her will, to check her ongoing worrying malaise - but it was too late. "Chemotherapy may prolong her life by two to three months, but at the expense of quality, this means that your mother would constantly feel bad, weak, tired, vomit, and I don't think you wish this on her."

"But it would always be two more months. Anyway, I read that there are many experimental treatments that would be worth a try right?" Selin said vehemently, close to losing control.

"The experimental therapies have some sense and are potentially effective if the disease is caught early. But honestly, we have tried to explore the different alternatives with your mother but she decided she does not want to undergo any kind of treatment, she wants to be okay or at least at her best for the time being and, even more so, she wants to be free to stay close to her family and enjoy her loved ones in the time that remains. Do you really want to do something for her? Respect her will, be close to her, be there for her. The last thing she needs now is another doctor because, believe me, the last two months have been filled with doctors appointment. What she needs is a daughter. Be her daughter, stand beside her... it's all you can do."

Selin turned her gaze to her friend looking for support, help, something else to argue. She could not believe that that was it, that there was no solution, that she simply had to accept what was happening to her mother as if it was natural. What could be natural about losing a parent? Her gaze tightened towards her disheartened friend.

"It's time to go home, Selin," Stella said. "Your family is waiting for us."

Somehow she accepted the fact that it was time to meet her family, but before leaving, the doctor picked up a brochure from a shelf and handed it to her, telling her "when you're ready, read this booklet as well, I'm sure that it will help address your thoughts in such a difficult time."

Selin quickly looked the title: *the stages of grief* and she wondered what she was supposed to do with that. The doctor would have had to give it to her mother, not her. She puts it in her bag and walked out, completely forgetting the brochure and thinking about how to deal with her family.

At the door of her house she was seized by hesitation. She turned to look at her friend "I don't think I can do it, I mean...What should I tell her? That I am completely useless? That I cannot help her in any way? That I am her disappointment?"

Before answering her, the friend rang the doorbell, and then simply said "you will find a way."

In the kitchen she found all of her siblings ready to accept her back with warmth and no one reproached the fact that she simply escaped in denial of the problem. How did her younger siblings manage to be so strong and to stay there? Of course, her sister's red eyes told her that she had spent that time in tears and at that moment, she felt weak and ashamed of herself. "Where's Mum?"

"She's resting," replied Amaia.

"May I?" asked Selin, meaning that she wanted to go to her mother's room and spend time with her. Her sister immediately understood and answered with a shy smile, "certainly, that would make her very happy."

While her friend remained with her siblings, she walked into her mother's room, opened the door and walked over to the bed sitting down on one side. Her mother's eyes were closed, but at the very moment in which she felt the bed move, and opened her eyes to see her daughter, at last, there in front of her. Her lips stretched into a smile. "You're here," she said in a weak voice, tired, her face pale. The only thing that Selin could say was "mum" before bursting into tears, long held in and full of unspoken words.

Her mother reached her hand out, resting it on Selin's thigh. "It's all right my baby girl, it's all good".

Selin stopped crying just to tell her, "I'm sorry mum."

"Don't be. It's okay, honey."

"But why didn't you tell me before? Why wait so long?"

"What could I do? Call you on the phone while you were telling me your typical day at work I would say oh, I forgot to tell you that I have a tumour. Believe me it was not easy for me to accept it, as it is for you now."

"Is not funny. You should have warned me right away, I would have come back and we would have gone together to the doctor."

"But your sister was with me. And I could never cause any of my children such pain, especially over the phone. And I also wanted to be sure that there were no alternatives or a different diagnosis. I wanted to be sure what to tell you. I am sorry you're missing important days of work to stand by me."

"Don't worry about the job, I don't care about anything at the moment, I just want to be with you." And in saying that, she squeezed her hand to communicate her affection in some way. "I will stay with you all the time you want."

"You know at first it was difficult to accept everything that was happening to me but now I've started to think that this disease is the best thing that could have happened to me."

"How can you say such a thing?"

"Don't get me wrong, dear. Obviously I am not happy, and when I got the news I was angry. Angry with the doctors, with God, with the world, with myself. I just wanted to scream and to understand why. Why me? Did I somehow deserve it? And then I started thinking about all of you, that I will lose my children. But most of all, you came into my mind. I will never see the children of Amaia become young adults, my grandchildren; I will never see a photographic exhibition of Arianna. I'll never get to read her name in the papers because I know that she will soon become famous, but I will not be there any more when that happens. And Stefano, the only son I have, I will miss him a lot, his joy, his will to live. His positivity is so contagious that the mere thought of him makes me be serene. But you, my darling, you're the one I think about most of all."

"Why?"

"I'm afraid I will never see you being happy."

"What? What do you mean? I am happy! Of course, not at this time. But I have a great career and... and!"

"That's what worries me, honey. You've got a great career and ...? You've always been a hard worker and that is something that I could not be more proud of. But you're not seeing the full picture. You've always been too serious and responsible. Even when you were a child you preferred to stay locked in the library studying rather than play with kids your own age. The point is that you should learn to play, to be silly, to make mistakes. Do not worry about being perfect at every moment. Give yourself the freedom to be human. When was the last time you laughed, you laughed out loud, so loud that the tears will slip out of your eyes and your tummy hurts, and you cannot breathe, but you cannot stop laughing. I never saw the joy, the joy that is in the eye of your siblings, in your eyes. And I am terrified that I will never see it in you! I do not want you to get to sixty, celebrating a great career, but with no one to share it with. When I call you in Milan, you tell me that the only time you go out is with colleagues just to celebrate a great victory."

"But Mum, this is what I like. It's what makes me happy."

"I know and that's why I'm so scared. You are not even aware of the wall that you have built around yourself. Do you not realize that only your body is moving in the world without a soul, without energy? And that bothers me a lot. I tried many times to shake you but every time you become even more impenetrable. At least promise me that sometimes you will have fun as well!"

"Mum, I'm fine! I don't know why you're so worried about me, but I can assure you that I'm happy. I have exactly what I want, I promise." Unfortunately her words sounded fake even to her own hears. She had recently begun to notice the emptiness that pervaded her throughout but did not want her mother to be concerned about her at all when she should be worrying only about herself now.

"Why don't I make some hot tea? Perhaps with some cookies?"

"Yes, please, that would be great! But give me two minutes and will I come drink it there. I rested enough for today and I really want to be with my family. Just give me the chance to get changed and I'll be there."

"Okay, in the meantime I will prepare the tea," and as she said this, she walked away and put an end to that talk about her existential loneliness.

CHAPTER VI

In the kitchen, her siblings and her friend Stella were in the middle of a lively discussion about some silly TV show and some C-list actors. For a moment, Selin looked at them and then herself with her mother's eyes and had a clear vision of what she saw: she knew that her mother was right. There was no serenity in her eyes. She continued to move forward in her life like an automaton, knocking all the walls that were in her way but leaving emotions out of everything. It was true, she had no friends in Milan, or rather, had many acquaintances but none of whom would ever open her soul to. Her only real friend was Stella, and only because she had always been very patient and had always left Selin time and space to be herself. How she could never have noticed that all of her siblings had a special light in their eyes that made them curious, pro-active, fascinating, alive. That light she had never been able to see it in herself.

Did she really wish for that kind of life for herself? Were all the sacrifices she made just for a good job really worth it? Did she really want to reach her sixtieth with no one to sing happy birthday to? Or sing happy birthday to her? Usually, she pretended to forget that her birthday was approaching so that she didn't have to face the truth that she didn't have anyone special to invite. She liked what she was doing but when was the last time she had cried from laughing? She could not even remember. For now it did not matter, she just wanted to focus on her mother and make her as serene as possible in the short time that was left.

When her mother joined them in the kitchen. even Stella threw her arms around her neck and kept repeating how sorry she was and how she felt guilty for not going to visit her in recent months. Her mother hugged Stella and after a while she only said "Enough with being sad! Now I just want to enjoy my hot tea in the company of all these young beautiful people. Enough long faces." And so, she sat down around the table and grabbing her cup of tea, she said, "well, what's new?"

The youngest sister began talking enthusiastically. "Stefano and I have had a fantastic idea, indeed a brilliant idea. Listen carefully! Well, I don't know if you are going to be on board with it, we thought the mood was so black these days, all sad, all depressed. In short, we strongly believe that it is time to change things up, so me and my nice little brother would like to organize a super mega party. In short, we could organize it in the country house where we have a huge terrace and, and... so Mum you could meet all your friends at once, and possibly while drinking alcohol, so you do not get bored with their continuous apologies for your situation. So, if Selin agrees, we could have the party in two weeks, the night of her birthday. It's been so long since this family has spent a birthday together. In short, I am the youngest and when I was ten years old, Amaia had already gone to university, officially engaged and about to get married and Selin was already living in Milan and my beautiful little brother had no intention to bring his sister to his birthday parties. In short, I have no real memory of a birthday spent together. Now we're all here and we could take advantage of it. Anyway, it only means waiting another two weeks. And using the pretext of Selin birthday. No inconvenient questions will arise about why we are organizing this party until you're ready mum.

I know, Selin, you have your job waiting for you but, at the most, if you cannot stay here for two weeks, you can go back to Milan and fly back to Bernalda on your birthday. Wouldn't be great?"

Her big eyes full of hope were pure white and bright light in the darkest night.

"Mum, what do you say?" asked Selin

"It is simply a fantastic idea. I am so looking forward to it! I was really feeling like a little music and chitchat. And you? Do you think you can come back in a couple of weeks?"

"Actually, I'm not going anywhere. I think it's a great idea." said Selin.

"What do you mean? Will you stay here in the coming weeks?" Amaia asked suddenly and curiously, as she continued to knead the dough for the focaccia that she planned to prepare for that day.

"Yes! Yes! By now the return flight I booked to Milan is long gone and I have already called Gabriele to ask for a few days off. A few days or two weeks are not that much of a difference. And I have so many reasons to stay. Firstly, it is so long since I've taken a vacation. And secondly, Ari is totally right when she says that it is probably more than a decade since we've spent a birthday all together or for me to enjoy a decent birthday without the stress of work deadlines. And thirdly, who doesn't want to wear a beautiful dress and listen to a bit of music?"

The youngest jumped with joy from her chair which dropped loudly on the floor behind her. She didn't even noticed it for she was busy screaming a loud "Hurray!"

"Don't worry about anything. Me and my dear brother will take care of organizing the most spectacular birthday party that anyone has ever seen. It's simply going to be fantastic."

While the youngest continued to share her enthusiasm, her mother approached Selin and softly asked, "But, honey, what will you do about work? Isn't it a bit too much for you to take two weeks off?"

"Don't worry Mum, I can take all the time I want." Actually, she was not so sure that it was going to be okay to take two weeks off work, but at that moment nothing would have moved Selin away from her home town.

"I am immensely happy my dear," and addressing everyone, she said "the mere idea of having all of you here for another two weeks is the greatest gift that you could give to me. My children, you sure know how to make me happy."

And the youngest returned once again to her mother's arms and shouted "I love you, Mum."

The days passed quickly, everyone was quite busy organizing this birthday party. Her father and brother took care of the physical part: looking after the garden that was no longer accustomed to welcoming people and was not hospitable. They had to strip away all the grass, paint the wall of the house, move all the wooden planks into an adjacent shed, and clear the boxes and other materials that their father had accumulated over the years and dropped anywhere. Ultimately, they had the task to create a large, clean and safe space in which many people could have the opportunity to enjoy a nice evening.

Amaia took care of preparing all the invitations and distributing them door to door using Selin's thirtieth birthday as an excuse and an opportunity to be together after all this time. They had decided not to tell anyone about their mother's illness for now because she hated the idea of people coming to her home to say that they are sorry for her and that would remember her forever. Everyone hoped that by announcing it during the party towards the end, everyone would have done so at once and nobody would later visit her. Therefore she would live her last months of life in peace.

They also hoped that by announcing it at a party, people were not going to really notice, or at least would not give the news that much importance, not realizing the gravity of the situation. They were going to only invite relatives, which alone consisted of a large number of people and a few close friends, of course, conscious that from that moment on, everyone would be aware of everything. Amaia also was in charge of arranging the menu which essentially consisted of a rich buffet of different delicacies. She would be the main one in charge of cooking with a little 'help' from all the siblings; but basically she was the only one who really knew how to cook.

The youngest, the artist of the family, was anxious to personally create plenty of wonderful and spectacular decorations herself. And apparently in her mind it was meant to be decorations everywhere. From the gate, at the entrance of the country-house, all along its length. She intended to give light to every single plant and flower her father had ever planted. She was unable to contain her creativity.

Selin was a bit of a wild card in the situation; she helped by supporting everyone. If there was anything to go to buy, if there was the need to print something or bring lunch in the countryside to feed her father and brother... that was her job! But most of all, she spent time with her mother. She felt like she had lost so many years by rejecting her and moving away from her that now she was determined to recover all that wasted time. And especially now that she no longer had a job, she had all the time she wanted to be with her mother.

Two days after they decided to organise the birthday party, Selin knew it was time to call her boss to give him news about when she would go back and she was a bit scared not knowing what to expect from that call. She knew that asking for two weeks off would have been way too pretentious but they had worked in the same firm for years now and she knew that her boss would understand.

After dialling the office number, Selin asked to be transferred to her boss's phone, and waited to hear his voice on the other side of the receiver.

"Selin, hi. I was wondering when you would call. There is a lot of work waiting for you here," he said in a tone that was meant to be humorous but his impatience was apparent. "Darling, are you already back in Milan? Will you start again tomorrow?"

"Well, Gabriele." That was the name of her boss who preferred to avoid excessive formalities like being called 'Sir'. "Have you got a minute to talk? Because, the last time we talked I wasn't entirely honest with you. I mean, I had to stay a couple of days longer in Bernalda because of a personal thing but it is more serious than I let on" began Selin.

"Is everything alright?"

"It's my mother. I recently discovered that she's seriously ill. In short, she has cancer and does not have much longer to live. The doctors gave her only a few months and, I mean, now she seems to feel good or better at least. She is pale, tired but well. What I mean to say is that for now, I will not be able to return to Milan."

"Oh, Selin, damn. I'm really sorry! I wasn't expect that. That is terrible news. How many more days would you like to take? Do you want to take the rest of the week off and we'll see you next Monday? I could give some of your cases to others and stall on the smaller ones."

"Gabriele thanks but…" and without even realizing what was about to say, she said, "…I called just to inform you that I'm giving my resignation. I will not leave my mother and Bernalda in the coming months and I don't know what will happen yet, but I can not work for you, nor live in Milan! I cannot live the same life."

"Wait, wait a minute! I am sure that we can reach a compromise. I could try to reduce your workload for a while so whenever you need it you can go back to your home-town. What do you think?"

"I'm sorry, Gabriele, I was really lucky to have the opportunity to work for you all these years and I have learned so much. And you knew from the beginning that I really wanted to be part of your team, but it is time for me to turn the pages of my life. Obviously, I will not get you in trouble by leaving suddenly so what I can do is work from home for the next two weeks and send daily reports and then someone else will have to take over discussions with the client and the counter-party."

After a moment of silence on the other side of the phone, she continued, "I know I'm disappointing you and that my decision catches you off guard. Believe me, it also caught me by surprise. I called not knowing what I wanted, but the mere idea of going away from my family terrifies me right now. The coming months will be all I will have left to stay with my mother and I cannot waste them. My siblings are free to manage themselves; one sister lives here, the other is an artist and can achieve whatever she wants wherever she goes and my brother has an assistant who can manage his bar until he is away. But my business links me to a specific place that does not match the space I want to occupy at the moment."

"I'm not disappointed. I'm just aware that I'm about to lose a valuable resource, one that never gave up until there was a solution to a problem. I'm sorry for everything you're going through right now," And after a brief pause, he said, "I will send everything by email today. I will assign you Carlo as an intermediary with our client. You will refer everything to him. So, two weeks of collaboration and then... it was nice working with you. If you change your mind one day and decide to come back here just give me a call, okay?"

"Will do, Gabriele."

"Goodbye dear and good luck." And with that, the conversation ended.

Still holding the phone, Selin froze for a moment in order to process what had just happened. In the space of a two minutes phone call, she erased all her studies, her sacrifices, the hard work in the firm to earn the respect and trust of her colleagues and her boss and get so close to becoming the youngest partner in the firm. And in just two minutes it was all gone. She only ever had one goal in her life that had defined each step of her existence and in the end she had fulfilled that goal.

So if she was no longer a lawyer now who was she?

The distant chatter of her siblings reunited and their voices full of optimism, made her understand that she would somehow overcome her fears. Somehow she was going to make it.

Unfortunately, she knew that it would be impossible to work from home because there was a perennial confusion caused by her little sister and her irrepressible creativity. On top of this, the grandchildren of her older sister were often there because her husband worked and she needed to keep them under control while she helped her mother to clean the house and cook and do all she could. Amaia was officially the second mother to all of them and, actually, in a certain way she had always been: it was a role that had always come easy to Amaia.

Everyone's main occupation was to spend time with their mother. It was unbelievable how after all these years of a cold distant relationship, there were suddenly such an imperial need to simple share daily talk with her mother. She was curious about everything that concerned her. Every aspect of her life, her past, her thoughts, her advice that all her children now required for every little thing as if it was law.

In the evening, they all meet around the fireplace and began to ask questions to their mother. That was the time of the day that everyone was waiting for. Waiting for her to talk and share her wisdom. For the first time, she realised that, before becoming a mother, her mother was a woman who had had an incredibly busy life. She had suffered, loved, hated; she had had to face incredible difficulties in her infancy and survived all this by turning into a mature woman, full and rich in experiences, emotions and people who loved her.

She still remembered the night when her mother spoke about the childhood she had. They were all sitting around the fireplace. Even though it was spring, the evening was still very fresh. With a cup of hot chocolate in their hands, the news broadcast on TV and their father already blissfully asleep on the couch by eight in the evening where he would remain until, as every evening, around ten thirty his wife would wake him up in order to go to sleep somewhere a little 'more comfortable'. That night, one of the siblings asked her how the experience of losing her own mother was for her.

"My experience was a little different. I lost my mother when I was very young. I was only fourteen years old and totally unprepared for what would happen. My mother died in a car accident. She went out one evening to buy pizza for everyone. My father was the one that was supposed to go out but he felt too tired, so my mother offered to go to shopping herself. The pizza place was only ten minutes walk from the apartment but on the way back a car hit her. I never understood what really happened. The driver said that she had come out of nowhere. The fact is, your grandmother did not survive the impact and died in hospital three days later. Straight after the accident she had entered a coma and she never woke up from it. None of us ever had the opportunity to talk to her one last time. I found myself to be the eldest of three siblings and a father who had been unable to bear the pain of the loss of his wife and had sought solace in the bottle."

"Mum, you never told us what really happened to our grandfather. How come we've never met him?"

"Your grandfather loved your grandmother so much. More than anything else in the world, more than his own children, and for him it was impossible to conceive of a life without her. He gave himself over to the alcohol. At first he tried to hide it and not to drink in front of us but as the days passed by he could no longer control the amount of alcohol that entered his body so he would often simply stay away from home for days preferring to collapse in the house of a few friends rather than go back to a house so full of memories of a woman who had been his rock. There were days when he would totally forget to come back home and we would not see our father for even three days in a row. I was fourteen years old, but I started to take cash from my father's wallet at times when he was at home because I did not know when I would see him again and I quickly learned to do the shopping and learn to cook. I had the feeling that if it was up to him we could have died of starvation. I didn't say anything to friends and family because I was afraid they will keep me and my brothers apart. So I would get up early in the morning, wake them up, force them to wash themselves and get ready for school while I was preparing breakfast. I would accompany them to school and go to school myself and then leave in a hurry to get them and go home together. I would prepare a plate of pasta for them and we would study together. When they would watch cartoons I would do a little house cleaning. Sometimes my father was there but for me it only meant that there was an extra person who needed to be fed before falling asleep on the couch and then waking up at night saying "I'm going to visit friends" which was his way of saying that he would go to some pub to drown his pain in dozens of bottles of beer or more. We spent about a year in this torment when I woke up one morning, went to the kitchen to prepare breakfast for my siblings and found a note that said 'I cannot take care of you'. Nothing else, no signature or an I love you... nothing at all. At first I thought that was written while drunk and that after a few days I would come back home from school and find him asleep on the couch. But after a week I had finished all the money that I had taken from my father's pockets and soon I would not have known how to feed my little brothers. I had to accept that I had not only lost a mother for whom I had not even been given the time to cry for but I had also lost a father who after a year of trying just decided to disappear for good and not to be seen again. I do not see, nor I have news of my father since I was fifteen."

"Have you ever tried to find him after he left?"

"I tried to look for him immediately after finding that letter. I tried to go knocking to some of his friends house where I knew he used to sleep at night when he was completely wasted. But no success... they did not know anything about it."

"Is it possible that he has never wanted to know where his own children were? If they were okay? If they needed help?"

"Apparently not. And even though I can understand his pain from losing his wife, I have been very angry at him because he could not see that we had lost a mother and because of him we lost our father too. It forced me to grow up fast so I have never wanted to see him again and he never came back looking for us which made my task easier."

"And what happened once you finished all the money?"

"I had no choice but to knock on my aunt's door, my mother's sister. She welcomed us in her home, but she simply could not cope with the expenses that entailed the fact of taking care of three young kids. She had two children on her own to care for. And I myself, I didn't want to be a burden to anyone so I continued to be the mother of my brothers providing for whatever they needed. After school, I became an assistant to a tailor from whom I learned to make clothes for my brothers as they grew up without having money to buy them. Knowing my situation, the tailor would give me leftover fabric from time to time and I also simultaneously earned a bit of money to help my aunt. I did not earn much but the little I was earning was enough to not be a burden to anyone. In addition, to show my gratitude, I was also involved in the house."

It was really difficult for her to be a child and suddenly become a woman and walk in the world when no one had taught her how to do it, clinging to the memories of the mother that gave her hope. And especially the excruciating pain of finding themselves suddenly without a mother or father and in turn become the mother of her two brothers.

Selin asked her if she could remember her mother, and what kind of person was she.

"Fortunately, although I was little, I was nevertheless old enough to have memories of her. She was a woman who really loved her family. I remember that she looked after us and our father with a unique sense of devotion as if there was nothing that made sense in her life outside of us. I remember her smile was warm and huge. It was a sincere smile of someone who was happy... and I remember her voice. In the evening, before I fell asleep she always came to my room to talk to me to ask how was my day and did the same with my brothers. She knew how to listen and when she spoke she was always upbeat in her voice that calmed me down and made me think that everything was going to be just fine. For years I continued to imagine that voice in my head to give me the strength to fight and not give up in the dark years that followed her departure."

Selin was increasingly upset as she heard the mother talk. How was it possible that none of them has ever be interested in her past? This woman had had so much to say and pass down to her children. Selin felt like she was watching her mother for the first time. Stupidly she felt for her whole life that her mother was just that... a mother, without passion or pain or desires or concerns but only a person that is available round the clock, seven days a week to meet her children's will. How wrong she was! And how did it take so long to see the truth? Her mother was a daughter and her childhood had been difficult, but in all those years she had never heard her complain about anything or slam in their face how lucky they were. Indeed, the only one who was always complaining about something was herself, the only one who seemed unhappy and full of problems was her. Selin felt like a parallel world was opening up in front of her eyes. Finally she seemed to be able to observe herself from the outside and realize that in the world there wasn't just her, there wasn't only her point of view. She was surprised that she never wanted to know more about the family with whom she had shared many years of life. Suddenly eager to understand the portions of the past she did not know, she began to ask more and more questions to the unknown woman who was her mother, taking advantage of those evening times when the whole family was reunited.

They question her on what it was like to discover she had a baby for the first time.

"You can not even imagine the immense joy that your father and I felt when we discovered that I was pregnant for the first time. We were recently married and had an extremely simple ceremony which was all we could afford. We got married at the town hall and at home we organized a reception for friends and closest relatives. Twenty people and it seemed to have everything in life we could wish for. Finally my existence seemed to take on a stability dimension that for years I could not see in my life. Being pregnant for me legitimized what I was for my brothers: a mother. Finally all the sacrifices seemed to assume a meaning, taking me to that point. I found out only later that the first pregnancies are always the most difficult. I was at the fourth month of pregnancy when I felt a terrifying belly pain, ran into the bathroom and found myself bleeding.

I called your father right away and went to the emergency room but unfortunately there was no help for our son who was not to be born. We cried both of us for days and days but then we sat down and we talked. We wanted, both of us, to have a family and that accident was not going to stop us from trying again. Having a family on our own was the only thing that would have allowed us to endure any difficulties we encountered in our lives. That, we knew way too well. And so we tried again until six months later the wonderful news that Amaia was inside of me and would soon become a beautiful baby girl. Imagine how happy we were at that time. Things had finally started to turn in the right direction. In fact two years later it was the turn of Selin and then you two were on your way too" she said, looking at Stefano and Arianna "everything was going to be fine."

Selin did not even know that her mother had had a miscarriage, news that the others seemed familiar with. That increased her feeling that she was the only outsider inside the family. This pushed her even more to ask and listen. She then spoke of her work as a tailor, how after three years as an assistant while attending school she had decided to start her own activity, working from her own house so that she could take care of her family at the same time. She began by doing simple jobs like adjusting the length of a dress. Until people learned they could rely on her professionalism and she began to make brand new clothes from scratch. She could still remember how in the beginning of her career as a tailor she had to go from house to house to collect suits that people wanted to make smaller, or mend after it had broken. She would carry them home and then bring them back as soon as possible. Sometimes, although rarely, she was commissioned to make an entire tailored suit from scratch. Oh, the excitement! In fact, over the years the number of customers increased as well as increased demands of more intriguing and fascinating requests. She had stopped only a few years earlier because her sight deteriorated more and more and started to struggle to keep the same pace as before. However, there were still people that demanded her, and no one else, to repair their clothes.

And then she told them how she met the man that would become her husband. This man that at that time was only a shy and awkward boy that for weeks had be staring at her, shaken, not knowing how to ask her out. And when he finally found the courage, they spent the best night of their lives together. Since then, they knew immediately that they would continue to share the rest of their lives together. But she was very vague about it. She was very shy when it came to talk about her own love life.

"Mum, how are your relationship with your siblings now? We have not seen them much lately. I am surprised! I remember when we were little they always came to visit us. I remember uncle Filippo, who often took me to his stable to teach me how to ride a horse and with uncle Andrea would help pick oranges in daddy's field. But in recent years I have seen them less and less, and even when I went to visit a few days ago they both seemed distracted" Stefano asked curiously.

Their mother clarified immediately. "My brothers are like children to me, I love them and we are always in touch. But life is hard for everyone and they have gone through, for one reason or another, very difficult years which they are slowly coming out of, but it's not easy."

"Do they know about you? Do they know you are sick? Maybe it was a bit awkward because we did not want to tell them and did not know if they already knew or not," Stefano insisted.

"Of course they know. They are my brothers and I could not hide anything from them even if I wanted to. Siblings are the most precious thing that you have in the world, one of the most honest and lasting relationship you will ever have. I hope you know by now that no matter what happens in life you guys are inevitably connected to each other and you will always be there for one another... but sometimes life takes you on different paths."

"Of course, who would ever willingly give up all this chaos. When my friends know that I have three sisters they always ask me to introduce them and with Arianna as a model I make friends in two seconds," said Stefano, laughing.

"But what happened to the uncles? Why did they move away?"

"You have to understand that our behaviours are the product of joy and sorrow, of challenges that life spreads on our path - and life has put them to a hard test. Andrea divorced his wife two years ago and did not take it well at all, he believed in family and in marriage until death does you part, but it was not the same for his wife and the worrying thing was that he had begun to follow the same road explored by our father. The road of the bottle. Me and Amaia we were often with him, keeping an eye on him and trying to give him the power that he could not find alone. He is better but sometimes he still has dark moments where he gives up and thinks he cannot make it.

A few weeks ago your father had to go to pick him up from a bar where he had sat for hours staring at a glass of scotch before deciding that he could not do it alone and called us in the middle of the night seeking support. Your father stayed the night with him. But he is better, he is stronger than he realises… definitely stronger than our father used to be and slowly he will come out of this dark hole.

And Filippo had major problems at work: the company where he worked went bankrupt and closed down and he found himself out of work and with a family to support. For him it was a really unpleasant surprise since for twenty-three years he had worked in the same company and it was the only reality he knew. He began to look for another job immediately but it took him so much time to find one and in the meantime they finished all their savings and were really navigating in ugly waters."

"And how come we did not know anything?"

"They asked me not to tell you. They really love you guys and still remember the way you looked up to them when you were little - as if they were really special. And you still have that look in your eyes every time you see them and they could not bare the disappointment in your eyes. They had enough disappointment already. We all knew it was just a bad moment and that we would all come out together and they believed that there was no need to tell you. But for me it's not easy to keep secrets from my family."

"And they could never disappoint us, no matter what" said Arianna.

"Ari is right, they are family and we do not turn our back to the family" confirmed Stefano.

"They were just afraid, because they had already lost so much and did not want to lose you too."

And this gave Selin the chance to ask "Mum, what about us? Did we ever disappoint you? I mean what can we do in order to totally make you proud of us? What would you have us to do in our future?"

"But I'm already proud of all of you. And what you do is fine. Of course, I hope that one day all of you manage to have your own family and have your own children and so understand how all this will fill your life with joy. But the only thing I really want is for you to be happy. And if what you do makes you happy then you just keep doing it. If your work makes you feel good it is all I need to know."

"I believe I forgot to updated you on one thing. I no longer have a job, I gave up a week ago. I gave my notice."

A general 'ohhhhhhhh' followed her statement and her sister exclaimed "but why didn't you say so? We all thought you were taking holidays or days off. But this means that you will not leave town after the party?"

"I'm not going anywhere. I will continue to work from here until I will finish with all the clients I had in Milan and with the things I was dealing with for them and then I will pass the responsibility on to others. After that I will have closed forever with the law firm and with Milan."

"What? With Milan? Does that mean that you will come back to live in our home-town?" her oldest sister exclaimed visibly surprised.

"I do not know what I'll do. I only know that for the moment I will take a long holiday and I will stop here and then, and then... mum what should I do?"

After a brief moment of total silence from all present, their mother cleared her throat and settling, a little uncomfortable in her chair, picked up the word "darling, I have to ask, did you do it just for me? Because I told you I have not seen you happy? I want to understand."

"No, Mum. Of course, maybe if you had not opened my eyes I would not have thought about it. But you're right, you're absolutely right. All these years in Milan I have never created anything: I have no friends, I have no family. I only have colleagues. And this continuous run for the job. I am a robot, not a human. I have not felt human for so long. I have not felt any kind of emotion. Now I need to feel alive. I need to know that, if and when the day comes, I will sit around the fireplace with my family and what I will have to tell them will not only be 'I worked and worked and worked'. And after all these evenings spent together, all the things that we talked about made me want to discover myself once again. I want adventures, I want emotions, I want a different present that will turn, one day, into a wonderful past. I never want to feel empty again." And after a moment of silence, she continued. "You, mum, you've done something! What you did was simply open my eyes. And I will never thank you enough for this. But now, now I no longer know what to do with my life".

"Oh darling, the only thing I can say is that at this time I feel so proud of you! I know that it takes a lot of strength and courage to start again, but you are young, beautiful and have an incredible brain. And you know what? I am not worried about you, in fact, quite the opposite. I was more concerned with your first steady job and nothing else. Now that you have found the strength to get in the game I'm sure that only beautiful and interesting things will happen" and her lips stretched into a wide and comforting smile.

Giggling in her mind, Selin thought about all that had happened since her return to town, she said "actually, I've never felt so alive since I've been back in town. And although it is all so confusing, in the end, I like to feel... I mean I like to feel myself, to get to know myself once again".

"Now you can be and do whatever you want," said her mother.

"And that's what I'm doing," said Selin. And it was true, since her return, she had already experienced the pain, passion, fear, uncertainty and hope, as well as the joy of finding her old friend and her family. She had never felt so vulnerable, exposed, and yet so serene.

A few evenings again and the inevitable question, "Mum, who's your favourite child?" emerged in the conversation. Arianna was the one among all that had the courage to translate that general curiosity into speech.

Between continuous laughter, she replied "how do I choose only one of you? You are all so different and you have brought so much in my life. I cried and laughed, and I was excited with each of you. There are no preferences, there is only a deep joy that overwhelms me every time I look at you and I think of the lives that you have lived and especially to all that awaits for you."

"But come on, there must be one that you like the most. Which one of us do you think of most often? Which one do you call more often? Which one you feel most proud of?" poked Arianna.

"Clearly it's me." Stefano took advantage "I am the only son. It's obvious that I'm the best thing that ever happened to mum and dad."

Among the general laughter and controversy of Arianna that did not found herself in the words of her brother, her mother took the opportunity to simulate a yawn, stretching her arms and invent a "I am starting to feel really tired, I am going to bed to rest" in order to extricate herself from the embarrassing situation that had arisen and let the children choose who was her favourite. But how to explain that a mother could not live without any of them and the choice was simply not feasible. Choosing a single name meant ignoring the joy and worries that all of them brought into the family in a unique and special way. With her children's voices acting as background, happy, she fell asleep.

CHAPTER VII

Only three days to go before the party. Selin as usual was spending her days locked up in the library with the computer in front of her and plenty of law books all over the desk. She had decided that her house was too noisy and busy to try to focus. The first day she tried to work from home. The day began with her mother continually offering her food; her father carrying crates of artichokes or lettuce and asked her to help her mother to clean them; Amaia's kids were often in there house to visit them and decided to issue a cry of joy just as she desperately tried to speak on the phone with a client - and she had to lie and pretend that another client was having a mental breakdown, showed up at the office and demanded now her attention. Stefano would usually interrupt her while writing a report to ask if the suit he wore would help him with the girls. Yet Arianna was, she had to admit, the most difficult to manage. She showed a huge interest in her work - sometimes she liked it too much and, probably because she had nothing else to do, she spent good two hours sitting in front of her continuing to question her in order to better understand what she was doing.

"Why are you looking at the civil code?"

"Because this is the kind of law that I'm practising."

"And what it means?"

"It means that I deal mainly with domestic discord or car accidents or fights between neighbours and so on. This kind of things."

"And why are you reading those old cases?"

"Because helps me to understand the decisions of judges in similar cases elsewhere. In this way, I can better understand what should I use as leverage to bring the judge on my side and let me succeed."

"But you also go to court?"

"Sure, if you can not find a prior agreement."

"So you don't go directly to court?"

"No, you always try first to reach an agreement that makes everyone happy."

"But you always wear such serious suits as you see on television?"

Selin tried to offer her to read a fashion magazine or watching a TV show but nothing seemed to distract her from the task of entertain Selin with a bunch of distracting questions. Fortunately, in the late afternoon she had to meet up with some friends otherwise she would continue bothering her throughout the evening. And Selin had to admit that she had almost lost patience when she asked "but why there are so many people who argue?" Honestly, Selin did not have an answer for that. Speaking with Amaia and admitting that she needed a really, but really quiet place where to work. Amaia reminded her of the library and that suggestion turned out be her safety net. The point was that she simply could not work at home. Therefore her new routine became breakfast at home, spending the day in the library (often simply forgot to eat for how absorbed she was in her work) dinner at home with the family, helping her sister to tidy up the kitchen, play with the grand kids and talk with her mum.

The first time she found herself in front of the library, she was surprised than it hadn't changed a bit over the years. It was a majestic building who stood out in the midst of two ordinary houses besides it. To get to the main door you had to climb a bunch of steps that culminated in a door in mixed ancient wood and iron supported by two Gothic style columns. The high ceiling allowed to have long windows that were gifting the interior with plenty of natural light. And two huge floors full of shelves with loads of books to choose from. Among them, the risk was to completely lose yourself and forget about the life outside that building.
But the nice thing about that place was that she could focus totally on what she needed to do without fearing disruption of any kind. She could also be as loud as she wished and as violent with the keyboard as she liked because no one apart from herself and some random high school kids was around. No one there to notice what she was doing. She was alone most of the time. Of course there was the librarian - a charming man probably around thirty, thirty five years of age. She could not deny having noticed him immediately. As, Selin was sure, he had noticed her. After all, she was the only woman to go to the library, at least for what she had noticed in the past ten days. And her younger siblings were even surprised to find that there was still a library to go to.

She remembered the first time she had set foot in the library and had wondered what this tall young man was doing in there. His muscular and light-skinned body, with dark eyes as deep as the night. Seated behind the desk, him. A real surprise when what she expected was an old man with a pronounced belly whom spit a bit while speaking. Instead, sitting on a stool behind the desk was this young gorgeous man with his head immersed in reading a book.
Once near the desk, Selin had to pretend to clear her throat to get his attention because neither the door open nor her stepping all the way up to the stairs and through the hall had distracted him from reading.

Not expecting to be interrupted by someone, he swung from his chair as if he had been caught doing something he should not have done. At the same moment, the librarian found himself speechless, lost in those eyes so great and so intense. And how to blame him? the last thing he expected was to have before him a young, beautiful girl with delicate features who looked as if she had materialized directly from one of the many books he had read.

After a few minutes of silence, the only thing he managed to say was "You got lost? If you search the clothing store is just around the corner" words said with a certain embarrassment. She found herself blushing and smiling at the same time to hear those words said out loud. And she wondered if she really looked like someone who desperately needed to buy clothing. Okay, she was not dressed in the most elegant and professional possible way: a pair of jeans of around ten years old fished out of her old closet and a red t-shirt with the words *I love rock and roll*, stamped on it borrowed from Arianna. Of course THAT was not her usual style! But considering she had left Milan planning on returning only after a weekend, there was not much in her suitcase. Therefore, she had to go back to use some of her high school staff, plus some staff borrowed from her siblings. And above all, she expected to find an old bearded and spitting man working in the library and not a young and quite charming gentlemen.

Back in the real world and in full possession of her mental faculties, Selin replied "No, actually I would like to use the library. I need a quiet place where to work and be able to consult law books at the same time. Do I have to do some card to use it?"

Still incredulous of the fact that that girl was looking exactly for that place, the librarian said "oh sure, the card. It does not take very long. We can do it right away - and it's free. I will only need your identity card."

"Sure". While searching for her ID, in her purse, Selin felt his eyes on her and her body temperature suddenly arise, perhaps due to the embarrassment of the whole situation, or perhaps because more simply, she was magnetically attracted by that guy.

While the librarian was busy inserting the data taken from her identity card into the computer, Selin wondered why she had not taken a better ID picture and, soon after, teasing herself for being so shallow. She had to remind herself that she was there to work. And she needed to work hard if she wanted to put and end to her current cases and doing so, put and end also to her work as a lawyer and to her past life.

The sound of his voice took her back to reality "Everything is ready. This is your ID. I won't need it any more" he said giving back her ID plus a library card "if law books is what you're interested in, you will find plenty of those grouped together in the third ward."

"Oh thank you" and said so, she headed for a table where to toss her laptop and purse and then go searching for a few books.

After a couple of minutes in which he stare at her full of curiosity, the librarian went back to his book, and things returned to normal.

The library turned out to be the perfect place for her. Only the sound of pages been turned mixed with the smell of knowledge. After a few days she also began to use the phone in there because no one else was around. She asked permission to the librarian first, whom clearly didn't mind what was happening around him. She had to do quite few business calls but rarely she received them.

That day, three days before the party, while she was writing statements on her computer, she received a call from her oldest sister. It was already evening and within an hour or less she would have left the library. To see her sister's name on the phone display, when she was soon about to go home, made her feel surprised and gave her a sense of alert.

"Hey Amaia, is everything all right?"

"Selin, you have to come to the hospital. Mum passed out in the afternoon and an ambulance came to pick her up. We arrived at the hospital just few moments ago and I called you as soon as possible. Arianna went to the countryside to pick dad and Stefano up. I don't know what's wrong. I don't know what's going on. Here everybody's running and no one tells me anything."

"Amaia don't worry. I'll be there in a bit," and so saying, she jumped up from her chair, grabbed her purse and ran out of the library under the astonished gaze of the librarian. Totally ignoring her pc, jacket and her documents, which were lying there in that library, on that desk, whit that absolute solitude and deep silence surrounding them.

Arrived at the hospital half an hour later, she reach out desperately to her sister in order to understand what did just happened. She look Amaia straight into her eyes and she began to assume the worst when she saw her sister face so frightened. She usually had everything under control.

"She collapsed in my arms, suddenly. We were in the kitchen with Arianna, chatted of this and that. She was a little quiet and pale. Suddenly I saw her slump to the ground. Luckily I grabbed her before she could bang her head and be seriously hurt. But she has never recovered since then. I tried to shake her body but nothing. Now she's in there with the doctors and I have no clue what is happening."

Her sister was so upset that she felt the urge to hug her and tell her that everything was going to be fine. Meanwhile, the rest of the family finally arrived. Her father and her brother had their clothes completely dirty of grass and soil which widely contrasted with such white faces - like someone who expects to receive the worst news in the world. They remained standing there next to each other indefinitely. Her sister had grabbed her hand and held it tightly looking for a reassurances that no one was able to give her. At one point, a doctor approached them and Selin could feel the hearts of all of them beat at the same frantic pace. Fortunately the doctor left not much time for suspense and immediately said, "she is fine! At this very moment, she is resting for a better and quicker recovery" a big and noisy sigh of relief came out of the mouth of all of them at once and her sister hugged her with tears in her eyes. His father asked to the doctor, "what happened?"

"Unfortunately, as we expected the tumour is continuing to expand, and her body is weakening. Simplifying, I would say that the body has collapsed due to all the changes that are happening within it. Unfortunately you have to be prepared and know that such a thing is highly likely to be happening again, especially because your mother has decided not to receive any type of treatment. At the moment, we gave her a sedative and a prescription for plenty of resting time."

"Can we see her?" asked her father.

"Of course, but not for long. She really needs a rest. Follow me!" And saying so they went to her room. The doctor showed them the door and walked away to leave a little privacy between them. Her mother pale lying in bed tried to pull off a tired but genuine smile.

"Mummy, how do you feel?" Said her oldest sister, approaching her bed and caressing her hands.

"Better, my darling. I'm sorry I didn't mean to frighten you."

"Mum, the only important thing is that you are okay" said Selin.

They stood chatting for a long time till they reached the most difficult moment - one in which they had to decide who would stay there with her mother to keep her company. It was really hard because everyone wanted to stay but decided that their father and brother were seriously in need of a shower and that her youngest sister was a bit too lively and active for their mother in needs of rest and quiet. Argument that she did not accept without contesting.

The alternative was between her and her older sister, but her sister's pleading eyes made her understand that this was the right time to step aside. They had decided that every four or five hours they would have swap shift. In this way all of them would have had the opportunity to be with their mother. Before leaving her, Arianna spoke up "don't worry mum, we'll cancel the party on Saturday. It was a stupid idea, you have just made yourself weary with the preparations."

"Oh no, please do not cancel it. There are still more than two days and then I will have certainly taken all my strength back. And honestly, I need this. I need to say goodbye one last time to all my friends," she replied begging.

"Are you sure? You are not doing this only for us, right?"

"No honey, it's for me! selfishly for me! Now go home and forget about it."

"Okay mum. Good night."

That night, for Selin was hard to fall asleep. She envied Arianna for her ability to fall asleep immediately. For her was enough just to rest the head on the pillow and the magic began. Instead, what Selin could do was staring at the ceiling of her bedroom, thinking of her mother and the scare of that afternoon. She had never felt so lost and full of fears. For the first time in her mind had begun to shape images of what would be her life without her mother. And it was a strange feeling for her. Especially because until a few weeks before, she had never seen her mother an important element of her own existence. True was that, discover about her illness had upset her deeply and put into play all the variables of her life. Suddenly, the things that had always been so extremely important, as her work, had lost value while the things to which she had never given any importance, as her family, had suddenly an immense value to Selin. All of a sudden her mind began to wonder what was going to happen from that moment on. She could not conceive the idea of losing her mother when in fact she had always refused to recognize to have one. Suddenly she had the need to know the woman who had been part of her life for thirty years and which she had never recognise as such. When she realized that her mind was travelling far away and that there was no hope of falling asleep, she decided it was not worthy even try it. In only a few hours, it would have been her turn to go to the hospital and relieve her sister from her duty.

Selin went to the kitchen with the intention to prepare a hot tea. She put the kettle into action and wandered through their book shelves looking for something to read. Something to pass the time. Her eye fell immediately on a series of abandoned magazines on the desk. They were all medical journals.

She recognized many of those. Those were all magazine that she herself had bought soon after discovering about her mother situation. When she was desperately trying to find alternative therapies that she could show to her mother. Probably, she had left than on that desk soon after getting home from her little escape. She had completely forgotten about it. One of those magazines in particular caught her eye. She recognized it immediately: it was the magazine that the doctor had given her to read when she went to see her a few weeks earlier. She had hoped to hear that her mother was not so bad and that very soon she was going to be fine. She remembered that the doctor said that that magazine would help her understand. Those words came back to her mind. She decided that she was ready to read it. Returned to the kitchen, she finished to make herself tea and sat down in an armchair.

She began to turn distractedly those pages until an article in particular caught her eye. The title stated: *a journey into self-discovery*.

"Mourning is a process that begins every time we find ourselves facing a separation caused by death, the end of a relationship, a sudden departure of a loved one. Whenever someone with whom we have a deep connection lets us down, whenever we suffer a loss, in our mind began to activate a series of defence mechanisms with the aim of gradually help us accept the status quo. The grieving process is long and tortuous. According to some scholars there are five stages to go through before get to the full acceptance.

- Refusal or Denial
- Anger
- Bargaining
- Depression
- Acceptance

Denial represent the first moment in which you have become aware of a loss. When, for the first time, that news comes into your reality - upsetting a balance that your mind had built over time. When the 'news' takes us too far out of our comfort zones our first defence mechanism in place is the denial. Initially, we deny that that change really is happening which gives to our mind valuable time to start getting used to this new concept. As our mind realizes that it cannot longer hide from the truth here is that anger takes over. We are angry when we realize that someone we love is leaving us, no matter the reason, that are pushing us away. This pain that we feel, our consciousness translate it as anger. Now we are finally aware that something important is changing in our lives. We are aware of this feeling of not being able to do much about it, to be powerless in the face of the reality. We are angry. We get upset with the world, with the person who is leaving us, with life, with God, with our friends that don't understand us. We feel powerless and isolated. We feel alone. The usual question is, 'Why is this happening to me?' From that moment on, something snaps in us, something that tells us that we can not give up, that something can be done. That probably our husband, our mother, our son, our best friend, that all of them actually have surrendered too early. They didn't take enough information, experienced enough, fought enough. It is the stage of negotiation. Here, at this time, we are actively involved in the situation, with the belief that something can be done, we are positive, we are fighters. We are confident we can change the cards on the table. It is not long before to realize that there really is not much we can do. That sense of helplessness returns accompanied by the knowledge that nothing can be done to change the status quo: our son really is dying, our boyfriend is really leaving - And so on! We are now going through the phase of depression.

These phases can be processed more or less intensely and with a greater or lesser length in time but it is important to go through all of them in order to reach the healthy achievement of full acceptance. When we are mentally stuck in one of the earlier stages of grief without being able to move forward, we enter the field of pathology.

We have to accept that the best thing we can do, for ourselves and for the loved one, is being present. Acceptance allows us to live fully the moments that life gives us without being overwhelmed by emotions. It is a painful process in which the final truth to accept is that a person you really loved is going to leave for good. The point is that before that time arrives there is an incredible amount of life to live and the life we live in that moment will affect the rest of your existence. A single traumatic event may disrupt your life and activate a change - most of the time is a positive change. It is the time when we face ourselves, we look at us from a different perspective. A perspective that we like and that allow us to become strong enough to let also others see that new shining light within us. It's a new beginning. A better start of a more complete self. The grieving process often proves to be a journey within ourselves, of who we are now compare to the person we were before the upsetting episode that turned our lives upside down."

Selin closed the magazine and put it aside. With her eyes now wide open and a cold tea completely forgotten in the corner. She was surprised to realise how much of her there was in that article. On one side she felt silly to be nothing more than a human being who had more or less predetermined reactions. On the other side it was a consolation to know that she could now give a name to those initial madness days - that moment when she learned that her mother was seriously ill. Clearly her escape from home, her night with those guys to get drunk and have fun represented her personal denial phase. There were various stages of anger, she had been over and over with herself for not being more present in all these years; with her friend Stella for not have noticed her mother condition before; with her own mother for not telling her sooner; with her older sister and her father for knowing and have kept it a secret. Obviously the bargaining phase was demonstrated by all those magazines and printed research that were left messy in the living room table. Selin believed she was still experiencing the depressive phase. Although in a softer way when compared to the beginning. But at times she still felt overwhelmed by everything. Especially when accidents like yesterday happened. When her mother's disease is so obviously slammed in her face and she still feels so small and helpless and she doesn't know how to deal with it. Knowing that sooner or later the acceptance phase would have come was in some way comforting for her. She liked the idea that there was going to be a moment when she could finally be there for her mother. She drank the cold tea, washed herself, got changed and took the father's car headed to the hospital.

She found her sister sitting at a corner of the room intently watching the phone while her mother slept in that little hospital bed: her difficult breathing and her pale face, with a needle stuck in her right arm connected to the saline solution that would help her to restore her energy.

"Hi Amaia? How's Mum?" asked Selin.

"For now she's stable. She fell asleep almost immediately. It has turned over a couple of times but she seems to be all right."

"The doctors have said that?"

"They said there's nothing to worry about. Not for now. They will held her twenty-four hours in observation and then we can bring her home. They said that she needs a lot of rest. But they also said that the tumour is expanding and are concerned about the speed with which it could reach the lungs. They said the moment that happens there will not be much to do." Amaia spoke in a low voice, her gaze turned towards her mother's lifeless body. Selin took her seat next to her not knowing what to comment. Maybe she was really starting to accept the inevitable. Casually she glanced at the mobile screen resting in her sister's hands.

"Do you miss them?" Said Selin, referring to the pictures of her niece whom sweet, puffy face occupied the full screen.

"So much. I was just looking at their pictures. In these months I have not been a lot with them and all I do is think about my children. And I think about how they would live now if I should die. They would think I abandoned them, they would think that I left them on purpose. They would not understand. My kids!"

"Do you mind to show me some of the pictures?" asked Selin.

Amaia did not need to be told twice, put the phone between each other and began to scroll through the pictures. The two kids were clearly very close to each other. They were always together and the oldest seemed very protective of her little sister. They often kept each other hands. And from what she could see in the pictures, the two were also very close to their grandparents. Here was a picture of Jenny who was trying to climb the legs of her grandfather or Miki who helped him pick olives in the countryside. And another where Jenny pretended to drink coffee with her grandmother.

"This picture, I love it. It was last summer and finally I convinced mum and dad to come to the seaside with us. They are definitely not big sea lovers. But I convinced them and we had the best day that all we could imagine: my husband and I made hundreds of pictures that day. Mum and Dad felt like kids. With the children they made sand castles, ate ice cream, dashed buckets of water against each other. I am happy that my children have had the opportunity to spend as much time with their grandparents as they could. To know them and feel the love they feel for them. "Selin felt a cramp in the stomach at the thought that those two little kids had spent more time with her mother in their short life than she had ever done in her almost 30 years. "They look such happy and playful children" said Selin.

"Me and my husband are trying to be with them as much as possible. We try to let them play a lot, socialize and make them feel protected - at least until life let us."

"How did they take the news of her grandmother been sick?"

"It has been difficult. But we said that their grandmother will soon be in heaven, and that even though they will not be able to see her, she will take care of them and protect them always from above. For Jennifer it was more difficult to understand how she could leave their grandfather alone. She thought about it for a moment and then she said, *but you tell grandma not to worry that I'm here and I will look after grandpa. So if she has things to do in heaven it's fine because me and Miki are here.* I love my kids. They are so sweet and full of love.

Here is everything okay, so probably I will head home in order to be there before they wakes up."

"Yes, go. I am here now. Stefano and dad will come together in just few hours."

"Need any thing before I go?"

"No Amaia, just go. Your children are waiting." Selin said goodbye and remained alone in that room. Herself and her pale mother sharing a room which smelled of medicines and pain. She was not used to hospitals and did not know how to behave. She tried to flip through the magazines that were on a small table next to her mother's bed and luckily after a few minutes, she was so tired that she fell asleep.

It was the voice of her mother to recall her from her sleep. The sunlight filtered through the windows curtains and a big chatting out of the room made her totally awake.

"Selin, good morning" Her mother was now sitting on the bed, eating breakfast. Probably a nurse had visit her mother while she was sleeping and she didn't realize anything.

"Mum, good morning," said Selin adjusting the chair a little confused by that short and dreamless sleep. "How are you?"

"Hungry," she replied smiling. "Would you like to have breakfast with me? I persuaded the nurse to bring me a second squeezed orange juice and a second yoghurt. It is quite good."

"Actually I am a little hungry and I may enjoy a yoghurt at this point" Selin smiled in response. She left the chair and sat down on a corner of the bed. "You gave us quite a scare yesterday mum. But fortunately the doctor said you are recovering very quickly. Amaia even said that by this evening you will be back home."

"Yes, indeed. The doctor come by last night and said I can get out very soon. And this is really good because I really don't like hospitals - they are boring. There is nothing to do here."

"Mum, did you hear also the part where the doctor told you to rest a lot and not to make any effort?"

"Don't worry, doctors always says lots of things but you don't always have to listen to them. They have the tendency to exaggerate."

"Excuse me?"

"However, I don't do much of anything lately. Your sister Amaia has forbidden me to do a lot of things and she is not open to discussion. Sometimes she treats me like one of her children. She has a good heart"

"She looks a lot like you."

"You think so?"

"Yes, totally. I see you in many of her attitudes. Always so protective and helpful."

"Oh, Amaia would do anything to help the people she loves. And she's one of the reasons why I am so calm about this cancer. I know she will take care of all of you when I am gone. No exceptions."

"And I will do my best to help her."

"How's the work, sweetheart?"

"I'm almost done, actually. It should not take much longer but for now I will take a few days rest. We need to focus on the party. I must say the truth - Arianna is very good in these things. You should see her! The way she gives orders around as if she were the big boss. I feel so sorry for dad and Stefano that have no choice but to be dealing with her most of the time. She's overwhelming."

And as she said so, her father and brother came through the door "Hello everyone. How is the queen of the castle feeling today?" Stefano exclaimed smiling as usual.

"Well, we were just talking about you guys."

"Oh really?!? Perhaps you were underlying the unique charm of the gorgeous and only males of this family. Because, if this was the case, I would have no choice but to agree with you."

"Actually we were talking about the experience of working together with Arianna."

Her father put his hands up and said, "she is my daughter so I cannot speak."

Her brother instead said "it is my sister and I tell you this: never again in my life I offer myself volunteered to work with her. She's like a prehistoric monster inside a tiny girl's body. She is hyperactive, dictatorial. She treat us as slaves. She is totally out of control. Can you believe that the other day she came to visit us in the countryside with car full of balloons and got angry like crazy because me and dad we had stopped to eat something for a moment. I am telling you, it looked like her eyes were to come out of her face. She began to screamed that we were late with the schedule and that if the party failed was all our fault. And every time I tried to say something she got nervous even more. Her voice reached unbelievable heights. She even said that now she was forced to stick all day around because she could not trust us. At that moment I would have killed her but dad said that mum would have been sad. So I control myself and she is still alive. And this is why clearly I am the favourite son."

"Clearly" their mother laugh louder.

"About that, Selin" said her brother with a soft threat in her voice "Arianna is waiting for you at home because you have to help her with the table decorations."

Her mum looked at her and in between laughs said "Good luck, darling."

"Instead of going back home it seems I am going to an appointment with the devil. That girl is tiny but incredibly scary when she wants to." And saying so, she grabbed her purse and once on the door she said "guys, take good care of mum and bring her back home all in one piece."

"Don't even say it, mum is in good hands." And saying so she left the room and went back home with the hope of getting a good few hours sleep but with the knowledge that she would have to work with Arianna to the preparations for the party.

Around dinner time her parents and Stefano finally returned home and they could all eat together and chat and get over the last twenty-four hours.

The other two days went by between frantic final preparations for the party and taking care of their mother. From the moment she came back home from the hospital it was a challenge between who would pamper and cuddle her the most.

Her younger sister even began to literally tuck the blankets like she was dealing with an invalid - and once she even tried to sing a lullaby but she was interrupted by a "no, please" of her mother -and the general laughter of them all. Her sister of course got upset. Her arms crossed close to her chest. "My voice is not that bad" she said. Her impulsive instincts convince her to anyway sing a song just to show them that they were wrong. They had to pull her out of the room. Everyone was simply really happy to have their mother safe in their home and not even those little accidents of craziness could ruin the mood.

CHAPTER VIII

It was midnight when Selin found herself awakened all of a sudden: light switched on in her room; a screaming family attempting to sing a Happy Birthday; Arianna jumping on her bed; Stefano continuously whistling and screaming like a madman; Amaia on the edge of the door carrying on her hands a birthday cake and her parents sang her birthday song with a big smile on their face and emotional eyes. Selin scared at first, it took her a while to be fully awaken and begin to understand what was happening around. Between those intense hugs that Arianna was giving her -how could a girl so tiny have such strong arms?- somehow she managed to catch her breath for a moment and say a *thank you*. Her mother sat on the side of the bed, visibly pale. Certainly she was not used to such late schedules "Happy Birthday, Selin. I hope your siblings didn't scare you."

Stefano interrupted them immediately with a "come on, lazy girl. Let's go! Get out of that bed. We need to go to the kitchen in order to eat this incredible cake. And if you're good, maybe you will even get a gift" he added with a promising tone. And turning on his steps he began to shove Amaia and the cake to the kitchen.

"Okay, okay. I'm coming. But how do you get all this energy at this time of the night?" Said Selin using all her energy to suppress a yawn.

"Because unlike you we are still young and, you know as they say, after thirty all goes downhill" said Arianna jumping like a frog, in her pyjama, out of the bed and, crossing their parents over, she reached Stefano in the kitchen.

Selin took her mother's arm "Mum, are you all right?"

"Yes, of course sweetheart. Just tired... but happy to be here to celebrate your birthday."

"Finally you made it", said her brother, smiling with bright and joyful eyes.

In the kitchen, waiting for them, there was a table set with cheerful decorations and packed gift. Many gifts actually. Her family seated in a circle around the table while Amaia kept herself busy lighting the candles on the cake and in doing so, she said, "before we allow you to open your gifts you must make a wish and blow out your birthday candles" said so she take her place around the kitchen table as the rest of the family.

Selin was the last one to remain standing and, deeply moved, she approached the cake "oh boy! I really don't know what I can still wish for when I already have such a wonderful family."

"Try!" said Arianna with her usual ringing and cheerful voice.

Standing in front of her birthday cake, Selin closed her eyes and tried to think about what she could really wish for in that moment of her life. But the only desire that her mind was giving birth was the possibility that her mother miraculously healed -that the cancer went away. But she knew way too well that this would have been just a wish and nothing else. She really thought about it and decided that all she wanted for her birthday was to have as many possible moments like the one they were experiencing here and now. Her family gathered together to share experiences that they would remain in everyone's memory forever. Opening her eyes she took a deep breath in before blowing out that shy little flame on top of the thirty candles decorating the cake.

"And now let's cut the cake that I'm starving. Can you believe that Amaia has prepared this cake early today and I have been such a good brother that I waited until now to eat it" exclaimed proudly Stefano.

Amaia handed her the knife and Selin found herself forced to make the cake into slices and distribute it to her siblings "okay guys, you know that I suck in the kitchen so please do not complain if the cake is mushy."

"Don't worry, the taste remains the same and that's what counts" expressed Arianna sinking her fork into the cake and admiringly put it into her mouth. The flavour of the cake was savoured with murmurs of total approval "mmmmmh .... mmmmmh .... so good. So so good. Sister you really did overcome yourself" said Arianna pointing to Amaia.

"Thanks Ari. How about we give Selin approval to open her birthday's presents?"

All too busy eating, they responded with a unison mmm ... mmm ... mmm. Considering that a yes, Amaia continue "each of us wanted to make a separate gift and make this moment a little bit more special. Therefore, you will have to unwrap four packages. One from me, one from Stefano, one from Arianna and one from mum and dad together. Here, open mine" said while fishing a specific package in that pale of gifts -a square, deep but small box. Selin felt excited and curious like a child. Were decades that she had not seen so many gifts to unwrap. Perhaps since her eighteenth birthday! And even then, she had not felt so excited as opposite to what was happening right at that moment. She unwrapped the gift and found herself in front of a black and velvety box. She removed the clip, looked up and the most beautiful necklace she had ever seen stood in front of her eyes. It had a thin reddish kind of gold chain that opened every two, three inches around a wonderful little stone, dark green in colour. "I know how much you love the colour green and it is so long since I spoiled you with something elegant. Even better, it feels forever that I last had the opportunity to look after my little sister. I loved spoiling you when you were a child, and this seemed the perfect opportunity to rebuild those memories" said her oldest sister with tears in her eyes.

"You have always been very special to me Amaia, you know that? I have always recognized all the efforts that you constantly put in taking care of me", said Selin.

"Okay, you two are too sentimental. Now why don't you open my gift?" intrude Stefano fishing his gift in the pile. It was a box a little smaller but much thicker. Selin placed the necklace back in the box where it belonged and grabbed from Stefano's hands the package he hold out "I didn't know you were that much into gifts, my sweet sweet brother" said Selin smiling.

"I am a man full of surprises, my dear sister" blinked Stefano.

Selin made herself busy unwrapping the next birthday present. She could not hide her surprise as she checked out the high-tech mobile phone that her brother bought for her. Taken by surprise Selin said, "I believe I already have a mobile phone! What should I do with two?"

"Two? My dear, you are very brave to call *phone* that archaeological find that you carry with you at all time. It is time for you to embrace the 20th century and all the comforts that hide within. There will be only one mobile phone you will be using starting from now on and that is this little baby over there" said Stefano pointing at his gift "You should know I am so embarrassed to show myself around with you ... and that cell phone. Believe me sister, very soon you will discover a whole new and exciting world of which you have not the faintest idea. You need to give to my gift one chance only and it will literally blow your mind. You will feel like trapped in a spider net -a beautiful and perfect design that contain everything you may ever need in life."

"Brother, my use of the phone is strictly limited to calls and texts" tried to say defensively Selin.

"And that just because you mentally belong to the Jurassic era" replied the brother. Mocking her, Stefano added, "believe me, give it a chance and you will be finally allowed to go out with me and my friends."

"Oh wow, if a chance to be publicly recognized as your sister depends on the use of this mobile phone, I'll be more than proud to begin to use it," she said smiling.

"That's it Selin. You have wasted way too much time trying to understand Stefano's gift. Now it's my turn" exclaimed Arianna while choosing between the two remaining gifts. She picked the largest package. It was really big.

"Arianna, this is huge! What's that?" Said Selin overwhelmed by curiosity.

"Come on, open it! I want to see your face as you unwrap it."

Excited like a child, Selin began to tear the paper apart as a wonderful canvas unveil below her eyes. Tears grew instantly, as soon as she realized what it was. The sister had painted on canvas the faces of all their family members. Her immediate family was happily staring at her from a oil painting. The faces of her mother and father were placed at the centre of the canvas, while the four siblings occupied each a different corners. Her father countryside was portrayed as background of the whole painting. Trees and flowers emerging all around their faces.

"Arianna, is impressive. This is by far, your most successful masterpiece. Sister, this is the best gift that I could receive ever, in my life. I would keep it close to me for the rest of my existence."

"It's strange to see my face on a canvas." exclaimed Stefano in shock. "Wow, is so resembling."

"Of course is resembling! My dear brother, you have not yet realized that I am an incredible valuable artist. There is nothing I cannot do" exclaimed peremptory Arianna.

"Thank you Arianna. Thank you, thank you, thank you. It is the most perfect gift that you could think of. But now, if everyone agrees I would like to open also mum and dad's gift. I am just so curious!" said Selin with moist eyes and a big uncontrolled smile on her face. That birthday was proving to be a big success. So over her own expectation. She grabbed the last box by herself, not able to contain her overall happiness. It was the smallest of all and the lightest. She began to unwrap it quickly taken by an irrepressible curiosity and, once opened, she found a key. Selin felt dumbfounded.

"I don't understand mum. A key? What is this for?".

Her parents exchanged a complicit look while Arianna exclaimed "if you bought her a car, just to let you know I request the same gift for my next birthday."

"Can't you see that those are clearly not car's key?" tease her Stefano.

"No, Arianna. No car!," said their mother. "In fact, these key is for an apartment. Quite few years ago, your father and I, found ourselves with a little extra money saved. So we decided to buy a storage unit where he could store all his work tools. But now your father is retired and most of the equipment has been moved to the countryside. Some equipment have instead been sold. Anyway, the storage unit is currently empty and has all the potential to become a little flat. There is even a little kitchen corner. Your father and I are very happy that you decided to come back in Bernalda for a little while and spend your time with your old parents. But we don't believe it's fair for a grown and independent woman share the same roof as their folks. So we decided to gift you of your own place where you will enjoy some privacy and is only two blocks away which means you will be able to visit us any time you like. Obviously, the space needs a good clean up and new furniture to buy. We will give you some of the spare furniture that we already have on the side but some other you will need to buy. So, Selin, what do you think?"

"What do I think? I think it's perfect! You guys are giving me a whole apartment. Are you sure?"

"Yes, yes. Totally sure. We have thought about it and we believe it is the best solution for everyone. In there you can stay as long as you like. And then, one day, if you decide to leave town again or move back to Milan the apartment will still belong to you. Maybe, it can become your summer house, where to spend your holidays. Or maybe you can rent it or, really, you can do with it whatever you want."

"Mum, dad, this is definitely the best birthday of all history" smiled happily Selin. "I would never imagine that I will be so happy to turn thirties"

"Enjoy this day, thirty comes only once. Now, how about another slice of cake?" said Arianna.

"Of course sister, let's eat. Even my stomach is now wide open. I am very hungry."

And they continued to eat cake and chat into the night. Even when the parents decided that for them was time to go to bed, the sibling continued with their happy, worried-free, talks.

It finally came the night of the party. As Selin woke up that morning, she rushed with her father down the stairs and two blocks down to go and have a look to what in few weeks, or months, was going to became her new apartment. It was perfect for her. Obviously there was some work to do, but in a short frame of time would have been ready with all the essentials for her to live in it. While her father explained the type of changes that needed to be made she wondered what else his father and mother had done or purchased without them knowing. Or possibly their siblings were well aware of family belonging considering that she was the one who had maintained conversations to a minimum in the past years.

They returned home with a mental list of all the adjustments that were needed. She left the practical stuff on the side for a bit and joined her sisters. They spend the day by choosing the suitable outfit for the mother to wear that night at the party. They tried different combinations of jewellery and make-up and get as final result a wonderful, mature, attractive and charming woman.

Selin, she allowed herself to wear the necklace that Amaia had given her the previous night, and that gave a touch of elegance to the simple black trousers and white shirt she had chosen for the occasion. And when they were all ready for the evening, Selin asked her friend Stella to take a picture of her family united. The first in a long series of photos that night would have followed: their memories!

They arrived to the countryside and her mother was deeply moved: moved to see the incredible work that in two weeks her husband and her children had been able to do. It was all clean and freshly repainted, with festoons and lights everywhere and tables full of food. Dozens of round tables scattered around their big porch -each decorated with candles and delicate flowers. Soft music hovered around. The atmosphere was magical.

Her mother could not refrain herself from exclaiming loudly "everything is perfect!"

Soon, the guests began to arrive one after another. They had decided to invite all the relatives as well as all the people with whom their mother had befriended over the years as well as some of the sibling's friends. Probably there were in total about seventy people. Some people had brought gifts for Selin. Most had brought flowers. Basically no one knew what to give to a thirty year old whom was virtually an unknown for all of them since she lived so far and for so long. The few times that she went back in town, she had always stayed only for a few days in which she had avoid them all. If it was summer, she would have spent her days at sea. Christmas was a time of the year in which she didn't travel, avoiding the chaos related to the holiday: she did not like the inevitable delays with the transports and the cancelled flights. She had travelled a couple of times for Easter but her communication skills were reduced to a nodding of her head. Naturally, she was not the Giovanna's son that people liked remember that easily.

She had to really appreciate, that night, how everyone had put aside their pride and pretend to celebrate Selin only to please her mother. And, after all, those gifts that she was receiving over the party had been made only as a tribute to her mother, and because of the respect they felt for her.

Selin was well aware of all the attentions on herself which made her feel inadequate and put her on a defensive state. But she knew she had to commit to maintain them on herself, at least until her mother would have been ready to reveal her illness to everyone: her task and her siblings task was to avoid her too much stress. She forced a smile and began to chat with everyone around.

But as she did so, she had to admit that after the first few attempt of talking about the weather and the economy that does not run as it should, the conversations became shortly to run smooth and natural. Most of all, as she gathered information about those people she reached the awareness that that was all -they were just people and not terrible monsters who wanted to harm her. The most fascinating thing was the realization that those people were really interesting, each with a different story to tell. She had happened to talk to three women who represented the jogging team of the 6.00a.m. Apparently her mother, until a few months before, used to go every morning, at six on the dot, to jog with those three ladies along a path that younger people use for run. And she did this for the past 5 years! Selin had no idea.

It turn a very fun conversation when they shared the several reasons they were all going jogging for: those who used it as an excuse to leave the house and avoid their childish husband; those who the doctor had told them they had a very high blood pressure; those who loved the old good fashion gossip. Her mother fell within the high blood pressure category and she didn't even know.

Selin also chatted with another lady that she discover was the nurse who had made vaccination to all of her siblings, including herself when they were children. Her mother, Giovanna, had maintained good relationship with the nurse over the years, and occasionally she would bring her an home-made tomato sauce. Apparently, the nurse had once said to her mother that she could not bare the flavour of the pre-packed sauce bought at the supermarket and that she had no time to cook a decent meal for herself. So her mum, time to time, will gift her with home-made sauces so that also this sweet nurse could enjoy the taste of a real, not pre-packed meal. Selin, was not longer surprise of how little she knew about what was her mother's life like.

She had the chance to speak then to another woman whom had connected with her mother through common friends. They connect immediately because of the love that her mother feels towards little kids and as she likes to have fun with them. Since then her mum would volunteer to look after her kids every time this woman would need some time off from being a mother of new born twins. That women had nothing but good words to spare about Selin's mother. Honestly, all the people in there, that evening, were speaking greatly about her mother. For what she knew now, her mother had always been a very active member of the community all her life. And she didn't restrain herself when it came to help people.

At that very moment Selin was chatting to a lady who had been great childhood friend of her mother before life brought them apart.

Do you know? When we were little your mother and I were inseparable. We would go to school together in the morning, studying together in the afternoon and go out together on weekends. We told each other everything. But then, you know, I fell in love with a boy who lived in a nearby town, and when I got married I moved to his place where he had a secure job. And as a result we began to see each other less. Meanwhile, your mother got married as well and the children began to arrive. I believe there was simply no more time for Giovanna and me to still be friend.

I dreamed to see you all grown up! Maybe you don't remember, but at the beginning of the marriage your mother and I made these promise to see each other at least twice a year. And she would bring you with her every time she would come visit. It was such a long time ago. I doubt you remember. But you probably will remember my son: you two played together all the times. Actually, the last couple of years my son came back to live in Bernalda. You know, after the tragedy that struck him he needed to go away from his father's town and rediscover the simplicity of his past. Anyway, I talked a lot as usual. If he knew that I talk about him so much he would be upset. My Matteo is always so reserved. But I'm so happy to see once again Giovanna's sons, all so grown up and all so beautiful. Receiving the invitation to this party made a tear come down from my eyes."

Selin was so struck by what her ears heard that she took courage and asked, "Ma'am ... Could you kindly remind me your name?"

"Pina, dear. Call me Pina."

"Mrs. Pina, can I ask you a favour? One of the next coming days, may I come to visit you at your house? You know, for me it would be a joy to hear talking about my mother as a young woman."

"Most certainly you can, my dear. It would be great to remember the good happy old times. I also do some wonderful almond and chocolate biscuit that you mast try".

At that vary moment a male figure approached them. "And here he is, my son! finally my darling." said that lovely lady

"Sorry, Mum" and behind them was the librarian who hugged her mum's old friend in a strong, full of love, squeeze.

"Honey, I want you to meet my best friend's daughter."

He looked at her directly into her eyes, not hiding the sense of surprise he felt in seeing her standing there, right in front of him.

"Actually we have already met each other in the library. Even though, I had no idea you were the daughter of my mum's best friend" and saying so he shook her hand, a strong and powerful hot hand that made her shudder. "To be honest, I haven't see you for a few days. I don't know what happened but, just to let you know, I have kept your laptop and documents in a safe place so that whenever you want you can come and get them."

"Oh but of course, I had completely forgotten. Thank you and if you could please keep them safe for me for a few days longer I will be really grateful. I will come back some time next week to pick them up."

"But wait! are you by any chance the birthday's girl?" brightened Matteo while Selin felt her cheeks blushing for the embarrassment.

Mrs Pina answered for her "yes, yes Matteo. This young lady has just turned thirty. The same age that you have, only few months younger. Actually, do you remember her? She always came to our house when you were kids".

If possible, Selin's heart lost a beat at the thought of those childhood memories that her own mind had efficiently removed -probably because she had done something silly, something to be ashamed of.

"I remember something," said Stefano vaguely.

"Of course you remember" her mother urged him "I remember that you had a crush on her. It was indeed your first crush as a child and whenever she came to visit us your face will enlightened of joy ... even if she ignored you for most of the time! So funny! I remember my dear that you would always take your homework with you and you rather urged to finish them instead of playing with my son or any other kid. But sometimes you were playing together and have lots of fun."

"Mum, please. Enough with the memories. You are embarrassing Selin."

"No, no, no, no ... absolutely not! Unfortunately I don't remember much of my childhood and I regret not having played more with you. I'm sure you had some incredible toys" to Selin's last statement Mrs. Pina laughed from the heart and she felt the embarrassment dissolve.

"Sorry everyone, first of all thanks to all of you for joining us this evening. For our family is a very important moment and I hope that so far you're having as much fun as we are having and I hope you all are enjoying an unforgettable evening. If it's not too much trouble we would need a minute of your attention" her brother's voice drowned out that of all the visitors who immediately went silent and turned to look at him -including her librarian. Matteo was still there in front of her with her mother who wondered what was going on. Did she knows?

"I'm sorry to interrupt," continued her brother "but now that all the guests seem to be arrived my mother would like to make an announcement" and holding out her hand grasped that of his mother, whose eyes were now so frightened as if her illness was now going to become real, as if so far had only been a product of her imagination.

Selin walked towards her mother to give her support with her proximity as did her sisters and her father.

When all the immediate family was beside her, they could clearly see their mother's face begin to relax. She could now speak the true.

"My dearest friends, I really don't know how to thank you all for coming here tonight to honour my daughter's thirtieth birthday. An important milestone that surely we are all immensely happy to share together. I'm happy to still be here, alive, and have the chance to enjoy all this together. But here, there is also another reason why I wanted you gathered here tonight. I wanted to personally thank you all for having, in one way or another, taken part to my life. For having enriched my existence with your presence. I wanted you to know how much I appreciate every little kind gesture you addressed to me."

Her little sister could not refrain herself from bursting into tears and throw herself into her older sister's arms, Amaia, while their mother continued to speak.

"Unfortunately a few months ago I became aware of the fact that I don't have much longer to live. I have cancer and all the doctors I consulted agree on the fact that I have only a few months left ahead of me. I wanted to see you all one last time to say goodbye in my own way and to thank you for all the beautiful memories shared together. I had a very fulfilling life and it would not have been possible without you all, my friends."

Absolute silence lingered in the countryside. It was even possible to feel the movement of the leaves moved by the evening breeze. Selin squeezed her mother's hand and realize she could not take that public speech any longer. She new it was time to diverge people attention from what had just happened -so Selin began to speak "this is why, our whole family thanks you for being here tonight. But now all we want, is for you guys to enjoy this evening and celebrate life with us" and said so, she walked toward the stereo and turned the music on and then back next to her mother where people had started to approach and surround her, asking questions and feeling sorry for the situation. But she and her brothers as they had planned, undertook to direct the people's attention on lighter topics and to move them away from their mother so that she would not feel overwhelmed by the situation. As expected, after an hour of fire, the night continued as it begins: chatting about light topics and fun memories while drinking beers or wine and eating home-made food.

After two hours spent next to her mother, managing all those guests, Selin felt the need to get away from it all and have some alone time. She left the country-house with the intention of walking along the driveway made of tiny little stones that after only twenty minutes of walking led to a cliff from where it stood a beautiful landscape. It was always isolated and it was her secret space.

As she crossed the gate of the country-house, and about to take a left turn, she came face to face with the librarian, alone, with his back lying on to the gate, an unlit cigarette in one hand and his head lifted to look at the sky. The sound of her footsteps woke him and it was like to see him coming back from another planet.

"I'm sorry! I didn't mean to scare you."

"It's okay! I just needed a bit of silence. Damn there are so many people in there," he said with an ironic tone that concealed an incredible sense of suffocation. Probably Selin was able to recognize that emotion just because she felt the same.

"You're right, we have quite few guest tonight. And I also needed a bit of silence -but this is not the best place to get it. Here you can still hear the music and anyone can walk by and interrupt you at any moment. I know a better place. In fact, I was heading there right now. Believe me, I need to escape this mess as well. Will you come with me?" she asked. In her heart she knew that the librarian would have being a good companion of solitude.

"I'd love to but I think you want to be alone right now."

"Don't worry. Rather than being alone what I need right now is not to be here. So, would you like to join me in my little escape?"

"Sure, why not" and said so he put his unlit cigarette in the pocket of his jacket and walked with her toward the dark. The first five minutes they did nothing but walk and enjoy the silence that grew more and more intense as they moved away from the music and the loud voices. Where they were going to, there was only the primordial sounds of the night to interrupt them.

"I'm sorry about your mother," said Matteo breaking the silence.

She did not answer but shrugged not knowing what words to use to express her feelings: pain, confusion, loss, loneliness. She did not feel ready to sail in that deep sea of emotions. To compensate Selin asked "I didn't know you smoke. I mean, I don't know you at all but I have been hours and hours in the library and I've never seen you take a break for a cigarette, or anything else, to be honest."

Matteo smiled "I'm not a smoker. There had been a time when I used to smoke but then I stopped. Nevertheless since then, I always continuously keep a cigarette in my pocket to remind me that I'm stronger than I might believe at times."

"And it works?"

"Sometimes," said Matteo.

"It's not that you happen to have a second unlit cigarette that you care to share with me?" replied Selin between hope and amusement.

"Unfortunately not, and I am not sharing my only cigarette with anyone," they laughed together.

"Here we are!" Said Selin, jamming suddenly.

A few steps from them, a deep and very broad ravine. In the background it was possible to catch a glimpse of hundreds of old trees that protected their kingdom on the horizon where the earth and the sky mingled in the dark of the night. The sky could be recognized only by the countless stars who lived there in that wild place, free from smog and almost entirely devoid of human presence. All around, only uncultivated land.

"It takes my breath away," said Selin aiming enchanted the horizon. "Ever since I was a child I always loved this place. It had the power to enchant and terrify me at the same time. It scares me to stay so close to a ravine but all this infinite calm and silence, well, is a blessing. Come!" And just behind them at a street corner there was an old wooden bench that allowed people to look across the landscape comfortably seated. When they sat down Selin said, "I was thirteen when I asked my father to build it for me. And he has not only built it but also customized it: if you look up this corner of the bench is my name carved in it. Look there it is" Selin could not believe that after all these years it was still there. It was probably a decade that she didn't go back to that place and it was amazing to see how everything was exactly as she remembered. "You know, sometimes I was coming here after school to relax. Sometimes even I would decide to study on this bench. I remember this place helped me to concentrate and to put everything into perspective. Also the evening that I learned about my mother sickness my first impulse was to run and hide here but, let's just say that on my way here I got distracted" Selin felt his magnetic gaze on herself and suddenly felt embarrassed. Maybe those words were for him just nonsense, maybe he was bored. "You should say something, you know?"

He distracted away from her and went back to staring at the horizon, and in doing so he said "I wish I knew about this place years ago. Maybe it would have helped me to get better faster." His words made her think back to what Mrs. Pina said about her son during the party "after the tragedy he needed to leave town". Who knows what was the tragedy she referred to.

Going back to look at her, he asked "This place is wonderful... So you are planning to go back to the library in the next coming days?"

"Yes, but not for a long time. A few more days, then I think I should be done."

"Can I ask what were you doing with all those books and laptop? You seemed always so focused."

"Well actually I'm a lawyer, or rather, I was. I gave my notice a couple of weeks ago from the firm for which I've worked for many years. But before to write the word 'end' I need to complete the handover. I would have had finished by now but given that in the past few days I have been so distracted I will definitely need to go back to the library. You know, right now I'm so looking forward to finally close with this work and with Milan and to have the chance to be alone at home with my mother."

"I can imagine. Is it that the reason why you gave your notice?"

"Yes, or at least I think. My job was in Milan and right now I need to be with my family. And in a way, I think it was time to change."

"Do you already know what will you do next?"

"Now, that's a one million dollars question. I have no idea but I'll wake up one day and I will know. Or at least that's what keeps telling me my mother. I never imagined my thirty years like this: no job, no husband, no children, with my mother who is about to pass away and me coming back to a town which I have always tried to flee from. Wow, now that is a change of direction."

The librarian smiled, "Well look at it as an opportunity for improvement. You know, I watched you tonight, you really have a beautiful family. It must be especially nice to have so many siblings. I am an only child and I always wondered what it would be."

"It's noisy" replied impulsively Selin with a broad smile on her lips, "but I would not change my family for anything. They are different from each other and all fundamental to each other. The oldest is our second mother, she is the most responsible and generous: she always put the needs of the family before her own. And she is a great cook. My brother is so charismatic and enterprising; never afraid of anything, he likes to meet new challenges. And my little sister, she is simply unstoppable. She has so much energy that, on her own, she could rule the entire planet if she wanted to. She has this artistic personality that makes her so unique."

"And you?"

"Me what?"

"How would you define yourself?"

Selin remained silent for a moment to ponder. Looking into her mind the words that could describe herself "I don't know. I mean, I know who I was: a lawyer who was about to become the youngest partner in the firm: a professional and a tireless worker. But now I would say that it is the wrong time to ask myself that question."

"Also because what you describe to me it's just a job and not your personality. Never confuse the work with the essence."

"I didn't know you were such a wise man!" And so saying they both burst out laughing. "But, seriously speaking, I think that my work and my personality have always been very confused in my mind. They were a single block. I have never been able to define myself without mentioning my job. Maybe that's why at this time I feel so confused. I feel naked without a work description defining me. I feel empty. I need to find myself again… or, find myself for the first time".

And that's how they spent the next few hours: talking and talking and talking. Abstract, lightweight and generic topic. They spoke of their childhood. She asked him if it was true what her mother had told her about whether they played together or not. And she was surprised to find out that he actually remembered. Basically from what she discovered that night, he had actually had a crush on her, so perhaps it was not so strange. "I remember that every time we came to visit your mother, often in the country-house, we would enjoy a meal together. Afterwords our mothers would request to talk alone and we would begin to chase each other around the trees and did every game that we could think of. We played often hide and seek and when we were tired we would sat down on the couch watching TV. I inevitably would fell asleep and then woke up back to my parents house. But it is normal that you do not remember anything. We had probably six or seven years at the time. But maybe you remember when you fell off your bike. Me and your sister were going around with the bike that day and I remember that you had probably just learned to use it but you were so stubborn that you wanted to go at the same speed at which we were going. You pushed yourself too much and you obviously fall off the bike. If I recall correctly you had lost a lot of blood from the knee that time."

Selin's surprised face could not be contained "I do remember that! That experience left me a scar on the knee that I still have today. I would never have connected those events between them without your help."

"Are you saying that you recognise me when I first came to the library?" add Selin out of curiosity.

"No, without my mum mention it, I would not have been able to recognise you. I did not know who your mother was. In the past decades has happened so much that it is quite hard to remember what happened in my life before then. I guess this is not how you had planned to spend your thirties birthday ."

"I know you won't believe it, but this is the best birthday I've ever had. I have never felt part of something until now. I had never been really connected with my family to this day. As opposite of you and your mother: you guys seems to have a very deep bond."

"If you knew my mother, you would understand that could never be otherwise. She would never allow it. And if you must know the truth, right now I'm back living in my mother's house. It is now little over three years that we live again together and, even though, the idea of it may feel inadequate, true is we have a lot of fun together."

"How have you been able to build this wonderful relationship with your mother? Is there a secret?"

"I don't know, the only thing that I can tell you is that our parents are also human being and a times this causes them to make mistakes, just as we also make mistakes. The important thing is that you understand that whatever they do, they do it for love" and they continued to talk and talk until they saw the sun peeking rate behind the horizon.

"Oh my gosh, but what time is it?" asked Selin surprise to see the sunrise.

"I would say that we missed the cake" comments Matteo amused.

"My family will be very worried and I also left my purse with the cell at the party. We must return. The last thing I want is to make them worry about me" Matteo got up from the bench and looking into her eyes said "Happy Birthday Selin." Her lips parted in a faint smile while her cheeks painted themselves of a deep, shining pink. Together, in silence, they head back to the country-house.

Obviously, as predicted there was no longer a party but only a great general chaos created by plates and glasses thrown on the floor, festooned plummeted everywhere, the buffet thoroughly vacuum and surrounded by flies which were trying to get the last remnant of food.

Selin and Matteo said goodbye to each other with the promise that Selin would soon head back to the library to take once again possession of her belonging.

Selin rushed at home, worried of her parents concern. The last thing she wished for was to make her mum believe that something happened to her or that she had run away once again. As she walked into the kitchen of her childhood home, all she could see was her siblings laughing and chatting and have a really good time. As they noticed Selin standing by the kitchen door with an interrogative face, her little sister comment with disappointment "Oh, come on! Why are you back already?"

"What?" asked Selin, not sure of understanding what was happening.

Among her siblings guffaws, Amaia tried to explain, "During your birthday party, we have heard that you left with mum's best friend son."

"Sexy mum's best friend son" interrupted the younger.

"Of course dear, the sexy mum's best friend son and those two…" she said, pointing in the meantime to the two youngest of the family "have well thought to make a bet."

"I betted you'd be gone for like a week overwhelmed by this intense adolescent crush" Arianna said.

"And I betted you would have act in your usual frigid, shallow way and push him as far as you could and now I have won and Arianna must come to Barcelona to paint a couple of portrait for my restaurant at zero cost" he added with a satisfied tone.

"What?" Was the only word Selin was able to say "but I thought you were worried about me? Where are mum and dad?"

"They are taking a nap. They are not used to social events and honestly not even myself, but I was having too much fun to hear these two crazy made up story about what was happening to you," said the eldest, "however, now that we know that you haven't ran away to Hawaii to live an exotic adventure I would say, well, I can go to my own house to finally sleep and hug my two children," and said so she left.

Selin, on her side, did exactly the same thing, not wanting to hear the nonsense that came from her siblings' mouth. But before she could walk away they stopped her "Then what happened? Have you kissed? You will go out together again? How was the kiss? Are you in love."

Her head was bursting for trying to follow the river of words pouring out from those two tornadoes. "Guys, before you arrange my marriage and choose the outfit for the kids, you should know that nothing happened. Nothing at all. And yes, I will see him again but only because he lives in our same town and, as long as I live here as well, there are quite high chances that our path will cross few times in the future. Now since no one is worried about my fate, I would go to sleep if you do not mind too much."

While Selin walked away she could hear the two brothers comment "Ugh she is so boring, she never wants to play with us."

"Do you want to play cards?"

"yeaaaaaaahhhhhh"

"which one should we play?"

Selin could not help herself as her lips opened up in a big, innocent smile to the thought of how much she loved Arianna and Stefano. Before to go and lie down in her own bed she decided to stop by her parents' room. Lately she liked to observe them as they slept, and see their faces so serene, which conveyed a sense of peace in her heart. It was like they were telling her that everything was going to be just fine. She stood there watching them for a long time. It was so hard to think that her mother was so sick when she was sleeping so innocently; hard to believe that there was something that was killing her from the inside. She finally went to bed and just before falling asleep, she murmur an "happy birthday Selin" to herself. With a smile, she fell asleep.

The next day she woke up with a sense of relief and lightness and that smile on her lips that had never abandon her over the night. She stretched and turned her gaze lingered on the clock only to realize that it was already eleven in the morning. It was so long she didn't wake up that late in the morning. She could not even remember when was last time that something like that had happened. Obviously her little sister was still asleep but that didn't come as a surprise. Arianna was not really a morning person and probably, knowing her habits, she had gone to sleep only a little while ago. When she went to the kitchen, she found her mother intent on cleaning around but as she saw her she stopped in order to make her breakfast.

"Thanks mum," she said as she sat down around the kitchen table. After a short moment of silence broken only by the sound of the pans, Selin added "Mum, I want to apologize for leaving in that way yesterday. I didn't mean to worry you."

"I wasn't worry at all, my dear! Your siblings told me that you were with Matteo and he's such a good guy. I could never be worried with him around. I know him since he was just a newborn and with everything that has happen to him. Poor boy! Believe me that guy could never hurt anybody. He is really a good person. I am glad you two are   hanging out together"

And there it was: his past! coming back up every time someone was talking about him. But what had happened? Everyone kept telling her that that boy had already been through a lot. She was incredibly curious to know what had happened but she felt really miserable in asking other people information about him. So reluctantly she changed the subject. "Anyway there were so many people at that party. Maybe we exaggerated. At one point it seemed to choke and I felt the need to escape. But if I felt like that myself, I guess for you it was even worse. All that feeling sorry for us, hugging us and ask us if they could do anything. It was too much! I imagine how much tired you felt afterwards."

"True, it was tiring. It really was. But mostly because I'm not used to staying up late and to participate in social events. In such a small town it doesn't happen often. But in the end I enjoyed it so much and I think I needed it. Hear all those people encourage me and support me and, you know what, I felt genuinely close to them. They were all people I had known for years, for most of my childhood. I know that sometimes it can be frustrating share the daily life with so many people in such a small town. Sooner or later, it gets to the point where you accept their inevitable presence in your life and begin to consider them an integral part. They become such an important part of your existence that your daily life is not the same unless shared with the people surrounding you. And now that everyone knows about my illness I feel liberated. I feel I can finally get out of this house and meet people without being afraid that they will read on my face the truth. Afraid that they could ask me questions to which I do not feel ready to respond. And the fact that everyone knows it makes me feel even better about you guys because I know now that there will be a lot of people that will give you a hand when I'm gone. I'm sure everyone will be here helping my family any time they need."

"Oh, please mum. Don't even say that."

"Honey, it's time to accept it. In a little time I will be gone. And if I finally managed to accept it, it is time for all of you to accept it as well. Believe me when I say that I am grateful -grateful for the last few weeks spent with you and your siblings. You can not imagine how great it is to hear your chatters fill this house so empty for so long."

"The truth is that I missed the chaos of this house so much more I could ever admit," smiled Selin.

"And, right now, I am not even worried about you, Selin! I feel like you begin to finally understand that there is more in life that career." Her mother said firmly. And after a moment of silence, "Do you have any plans for today?"

"In theory I should go back to the library to take back my pc and to conclude the final details of my old job. Honestly I don't really feel like working today. I think I'll take a day off and... Do you know what I really want to do? Wake my sisters up and spend the afternoon shopping with all the girls of this family. We've never done something like that for as long as I can remember." Selin enthusiasm was growing more and more at every words "Mum, I do believe you could use some new clothes in your wardrobe and maybe trash some of your old staff. I swear it won't hurt you to spend some money for yourself. You and dad have spent all your savings paying for my study and I think it's time for me to return the favour. And obviously we will also buy something for dad and Stefano. What do you think? Come on, I really want to spend a bit of money today! Let's do it!" Without giving her mother the chance to answer and try to persuade her in saving her money, Selin stood up and said, "You call Amaia and tell her to get it ready by two o'clock, after lunch seems a reasonable time. I'm going to wake Arianna up and I see what she thinks of my plan for the day.

How she imagined the younger sister was not at all happy to be woken up after a little over two hours of sleep but know that Selin was willing to spend lots of her money to buy them clothes convinced that new and free clothes were worth the lack of sleep. And basically she could always come back to sleep again after the shopping.

And so they did. Her youngest sister was probably the one that most appreciated the clothes shopping while her older sister did nothing but complain of such a waste of money as they forced her to buy something for herself. But, at the same time, Amaia left herself be overwhelmed by the magic of the shopping when it came to buy something for her husband. There was so much sweetness and tenderness in her eyes that showed all the love she felt for the man with whom she had shared almost her whole life.

And so did her mother "Your father needs new shoes for the countryside. The one is using right now are a disaster. Every time I see them I just wish I could throw them in the garbage," said at one point her mother and was so sweet to see that she was beginning to get carried away by the general enthusiasm.

"Well, mother tonight you will finally be able to make your dream come true and throw dad's shoes in the bin," said the youngest hugging her from behind.

And so the father got a new pair of shoes, two pairs of jeans and a simple pullover to use every day. Her brother got a shirt, a tie and a belt. The older sister got forced to buy a skirt, but then became impossible to convince her to spend further money for herself. Their mother at least accepted a skirt and shirt together. The younger sister was torn between three dresses that eventually took all. Selin chose a simple green summer dress but with a decidedly sensual end result: and that it will well match with the necklace received as present for her birthday. It had been so long since she bought something that she didn't want to use at work but only for herself. Something to remember that she was not only a lawyer but also a woman. Now a well growing up woman.

It was amazing the herself she was discovering lately. Discover that she could be relaxed and fragile and that all this was fine. Discover that she didn't need to be strong and independent at all times. Discover that she didn't need to feel in a courtroom in every moment of her life or be professional every minutes for customers and colleagues. She could finally be carefree. She could finally be a woman. She could finally be whatever she wanted to be. And whatever her choice was, it was fine! For that feeling of liberation she had to thank her mother for having finally made it clear that she would have loved her anyway, whoever she was.

Eventually the two planned hours of shopping became almost five and then they ultimately got back home to show their shopping to the rest of the family.

As expected, her father, as Amaia, took a while to convince himself that it was okay once in a while to spend money on themselves, which was even therapeutic. The brother was so committed to open his gifts that he did not even notice the father's comments.

It was in that very moment that Selin finally felt like she finally started to heal, to find her voice: she was not a lawyer - that was only a job.

So who was she? She felt that at last in her heart were forming words describing herself as a daughter, a sister, a friend. Maybe she was boring, like Arianna liked to define her. Maybe at times she appeared a little snob like Stefano scolded her from time to time. She knew how to listen and how to say thank you and appreciate the warmth and love that surrounded her. She could be generous and sweet if circumstances permitted. She could be a bit shy but also impulsive and determined. She had no problems to appreciate her body as it was and she finally began to give also value to her soul.

That night they all went to bed early again exhausted by the intense days that were experiencing recently.

She woke up, once again, with that brand new sense of joy and the desire to do something that meant taking care of her family. After the usual breakfast with her mother, Selin called Amaia asking if she felt like doing some rural cleaning. Amaia admitted she was thinking of doing exactly the same. That was how the two oldest sisters of the family decided to pack lunch and spend the whole day in the country house doing cleaning. Shortly after Amaia grabbed her car and drove the two of them into the countryside. Dad was already there trying to figure out how to organize all the dishes and trays laying around.

"Hi dad," said Selin.

"Hey girls, what are you doing here?" asked her father, interrupting whatever he was doing.

"We came to take care of the same thing you're dealing with right now" smiled Selin "don't worry dad, let the women handle this kind of job. I guess you already have a lot to do with your countryside to have to be worry also about cleaning."

"Indeed, I have so many tomatoes and zucchini to harvest, then I have to water everything and dig a part of land in order to plant new seeds."

"Exactly what I thought. Go on and do whatever you need to do. Me and Amaia will take care of making any trace of last night party disappear."

"Selin, I'm going to storage the lunch boxes in the fridge before it goes off. Do me a favour and begins to pull out of the back seat those big, blacks garbage bags. I'll be right back!" said Amaia.

And within minutes they were at work. They organized three bags of garbage: one for the plastic, one for the broken glass and one for paper, plus more little containers for the organic waste. Although between people and insects it was almost all gone. Furthermore they organized a trolley on which to put the dirty dishes that they would have washed in the end. They had to admit that the two of them were really fast. A few hours were enough to throw everything into the bags and throwing large buckets of water very quickly on the floor in order to wash that big patio. The two sisters relaxed then while washing dishes: Amaia decided that she preferred to wash the dishes and Selin got the task of drying them.

"How long it ha been since the last time we have spent some quality time together, just the two of us?" asked Selin.

"Oh my gosh, I believe is an eternity. Unfortunately we only had one and a half year of been alone before Stefano came into the family. Afterwords life has always been very chaotic. We have a very big family. And, honestly, since you were little you always preferred to just stay on your own or with your friends. You have always avoided being in the household. And as soon as you had the chance you moved to Milan to study. The only real time we had between us was when I helped with homework during primary and middle school, then your friend Stella had taken my place. But when we could spend some time together was just beautiful."

"I'm sorry Amaia, I know it is not easy to have me as a sister."

"Adolescence is not an easy time for anyone. But during adolescence, however, people makes choices, it doesn't matter if they are right or wrong choices -you choose and when you become an adult you are forced to accept the consequences of those choices."

"How come you haven't felt the need to get away from our home-town as I did."

"I didn't need to get away because all I wanted from life was right here at my fingertips."

"But there is one thing I don't understand. Stefano and Arianna also they have left home and live far away but the feeling that I get from it is different. It is like mum is not angry at them at all while I always had an hard time because of my decision to live town."

"May I remind you that Stefy and Ari live in faraway places not because they don't want to live here, not because they don't want to be with their family. Our siblings live abroad only because over there they have the opportunity to express their full potential. Something that they could not have done by staying in a small town. And don't think mum is mad at you, not at all. She is only sad because she doesn't understand what she could have possibly done to you to make you hate her so much. Remember Selin that I was right there the night you left for college. Do you remember?"

And how could she forget that night. Her suitcases ready and for some stupid reason she was once again arguing with her mother. Oh yeah, she remembers, her mother just had asked her to take an extra sweater because the North of Italy could get really cold during the winter. Selin began to yell at her that she was glad that she could finally leave that lost place and that lousy family. "*I do not want to see you ever again. As long as I live I will not set foot in this shitty town.*" It was the first time that she had said something like that out loud and straight to her mum's face.

Her mother stood there in silence, without saying a word.

Without talking to each other, they got into the car, she set then on the train and left for college. Her first time leaving her family! She repent those words immediately after saying them. She knew she had crossed an invisible line in the relationship between her and her mother but she was too proud to admit her fault.

"You were gone out to college but we were still here. Having to pick up the pieces of what you had done. Our mother never told you, but that night she came home and she burst into tears and cried every night since then until you finally decide to call her from Milan. She spent a whole month crying before you finally decided to answer one of mum's calls. We all tried to call you but the only one who could put some sense into your brain was Stefano whom has always been special to you and the only one you will have given your life for. He would have go to our mum and tell her that you were fine, that you were getting settle and start to follow your first classes. Thanks to him, mum was able to spend some quiet night instead of die of a broken heart. And even after you two start speaking again, there were never an apology, never an 'I'm sorry'. Your parents were paying the university for you, they were paying your life in Milan, your food, your books, your clothes and you... you treated them as rags. And despite everything that has happened mum was never really mad at you. She was sad, her heart was breaking but, even though, the only thing she kept doing every day over the last decade was trying to get closer to you.

   She was not angry, but I was. I am. You left me. Sooner after also Stefano and Arianna were gone but I was here. Dad and I were here to pick up the pieces of a woman that you had destroyed. We were having to listen to mum worrying as hell every time you did not answer the nth call and she thought that maybe you had a car accident rather than admit that her daughter was just a selfish opportunist. You had to find out that your mother is going to die before you really realize to be her daughter. I'm happy for mum who is finally able to spend time with you and talk to you as we have always hoped would happen. And I accept your presence because I want mum to finally be happy. But Selin, lets be honest, you can not expect to come back and have everyone ready to welcome you back, forget everything and tossed their arms at you. Ten years ago, I could justify you saying that you were still in the adolescent stage. But seven years ago? five years ago? Three years ago? When you went away you also left me. And my whole life I did nothing but protect and care for you as if you were my own daughter and not just my sister."

"Amaia I'm so sorry." Selin was pale in her face, with tears in her eyes "I didn't realize."

"I know, Selin. You've always been selfish and unable to see beyond yourself." Amaia continued washing dishes with an increasing anger.

"Tell me what can I do to make you forgiving me and I will do it. I realize that, in the past years, I wasn't a good sister or a good daughter. But, for what it's worth, I am here now and you got to give me a chance."

"The past is the past! Simply try to make mum happy for the next few months of her life -it is all I ask. And don't worry about me, I will learn with time to make peace with all that's happened." They finished washing the dishes in silence: Amaia trying to calm her anger and Selin trying to digest the words heard from someone who had always taken for granted. She had never focused on the real consequences of her actions. How she could have been so selfish all those years? Would she even have a relationship with her family if her mother hadn't got sick? Did she only just changed because her mother was dying? She felt a tremendous grip on her heart at the sound of Amaia's words that, as a condemnation, were still repeating in her head.

The noisy thoughts of the two sisters were interrupted by the sound of a horn, and the voice of their brother screaming "Everyone ready to eat?".
Arianna quickly got out and stood ahead of them, "you haven't eat already, haven't you?".

Stefano in the meanwhile helped their mother out of the car.

Selin surprised asked "what are you guys doing here?"

"We realized we didn't want to eat only the three of us alone. It seemed too sad and too quiet, so we decided that taking a little fresh air would not hurt. And then we had to come and check you were really cleaning up the countryside and not just chat all the time. So how's it going?" add Arianna

"Actually, we're almost done. We just have to finish washing those dishes and it's all done," said Amaia smiling towards Arianna motherly.

"Cool, we will start to prepare the table for lunch. Stefanoooooo …" Arianna shouted to her brother "prepare the table, they have almost finished" and turning to the two sisters, "where is daddy?"

"He is down there watering the plants," said Amaia pointing towards a further point behind trees "Go and call him. He must be so hungry."

Arianna turned to run toward the open country when it rolled over in her tracks "Selin, are you all right? You look thoughtful! Something bothering you?"

Selin put on her best smile and said, "everything is just great Ari, I was just lost in my thoughts."

"Are you still thinking about that gorgeous librarian, eh! Lucky you, I have the positive feeling that sooner or later he will ask you out. I have a special sense for these things." And turning back once again she began to run toward the garden of which her father always took great care. "Dad, Dad, where are you? Dad, times to eat" and the wind carried her screams away from audible ears.

Taking advantage of a moment of privacy between the two sisters, Amaia said "I realize that I was brutal in the way I talked to you before and I'm sorry. I never wanted to tell you what I said, I always thought I'd brought my thoughts with me to the grave. I don't know what came into me. But the damage is done. Can we try to bury the hatchet and make sure that the rest of the family does not realize anything? Can we?"

"Don't worry Amaia, no one will know about our conversation. But I promise you one thing, what happened in the past will not happen again, and in some way I will be able to make it up to you and to mum for the person I was." Said so, they finished to clean up dishes and reached their family on the patio where Stefano had begun to pour wine while their mother displayed tray of food in the middle of the table: eggplant parmesan, potato pizza, fried zucchini and more... Plus Amaia took from the fridge the rice salad she had prepared for the two of them in the morning.

"Mum, but when did you find the time to prepare everything?" Selin asked worried that that amount of work had required from her way too much energy.

"Actually I have not done much. I mostly coordinated the operations."

Stefano, full of enthusiasm interrupted them "It's all been done by me and Ari. Can you believe it? Arianna in the kitchen" and among the general laughter and obvious disappointment on the Arianna's face, whom clearly overestimated her culinary skills, continued, "Mum told us what we needed to do and we did it. In no time at all, everything was ready."

"And the result is amazing. I was the first to be surprised of what those two can achieved when they are together" said proud their mother. "Yet girls, you also did an outstanding job. No one would ever think that only the day before yesterday in this exactly spot there was an incredible party."

And they carry on enjoying their food until the plates were completely empty.

CHAPTER IX

The next day Selin decided it was time to put an end to her former life. It was time to close her former employment relationship in order to devote herself exclusively to her family. It was time to get back to the library one last time.

On the one hand, Selin was determined to close the chapter 'work' and even more she wanted to retrieve her computer and her notes. On the other hand the very idea of returning to the library made her feel full of anxiety and agitation. She was nervous. Not wanting too, she did nothing but think of Matteo: the time spent together and the synchrony felt with him, as it was natural to stand by him. And, even more, all these recriminations made her feel guilty. Guilty because her mind suppose to be one hundred percent immersed in family traumas. Guilty because she had thrown away the last ten years of her life to take care of her loved ones. Guilty because the last thing she suppose to focus on were boys... yet more than once her mind had developed the thought of the two of them as a couple, immersed in a romantic and intense relationship. His personality intrigued her greatly and his mind was fascinating for her.

Furthermore, he knew how to be extremely closed and introverted and most of the time it was impossible to try to interpret his thoughts.

However, she picked up that little courage left in her and went into the library but unfortunately for her could not prevent her face from blushing when she saw him, as usual, behind the counter with eyes bent on yet another book. Her heart skipped a beat when him, looking up from his book and realizing who was the person standing in front of him, he address her a warm and intense smile.

"You're here," he said.

In his head Selin wondered why that guy had the ability to make her feel like a high-school teenager.

"Hello," she said. "I see you've started reading a new book. If I'm not mistaken, last week your reading was Moby Dick, but today is The Count of Monte Cristo."

"Yes, new week, new book" he smiled at her "in fact I have already read most of these books in the past but, now and then, I'm glad to go over them once again and find that there is always something new that I haven't noticed in the previous reading. However, I have all your stuff right here. Hold on! I didn't expect for you to be back so soon. How are you? Are you going straight back home?"

"Oh, thank you for keeping my things aside. I am well and, actually, if it's not a problem, today I would stop here to work. I think still a couple of days and I should be done. Right now, I really want to finish as soon as possible."

"Take all the time you need," he said, smiling.

The only thing she could think of was that, that day, it was going to be very hard to focus on her work. But in the end she let herself be overwhelmed by something that had become over the years automatic for her. As a second nature! Going to a all new speed she managed to sort out most of her work. She called her boss telling him that the next day would officially be the last day of collaboration. That her work at Bros & Brothers, after all these years, was reaching an ending point. Following the voice in her head that was telling her that, that one, was probably the last time she was doing that very same job, she began to travel back in time. She was only twenty-four and with a unique stubbornness. After much insistence, she had finally managed to get an interview inside the Bros & Brothers firm. She knew she would have done anything to get into that firm. Their company's policy was not to hire new graduates -and this what she was. She had graduated only a week before with zero practical experience behind her and many confusing and, at times, contradictory theories filling her head. But she loved the law: she had spent many sleepless nights studying cases and more than once she had fallen asleep on that big Civil Code that after only a few months into the university had become her shadow and she had carried it everywhere with her. A foot inside the firm and she knew that this was the place she wanted to spend the thousand following days, and some of the evenings. She had studied the origins, all the cases they were busy with and she knew the name and surname of all the people working in there. She was deeply prepared for that interview. She really wanted to be part of that reality. And she made it.

But even in her wildest dreams she wouldn't dare to imagine, six years later, to be already considered ready to be promoted partner -and only fewer would have thought of having to give up this opportunity. Gabriele had become family to her, that's why she knew he understood and accepted her decision.

"Selin perhaps for a while we won't be in touch, but this does not mean that one day our paths may not cross again. Remember that the world is smaller than we can ever imagine," said Gabriele with his tone always a bit fatherly, always a little mysterious of who knows answers before questions are asked.

She ended the conversation with a sense of relief and a slightly hope that the words of Gabriele could one day become reality. She placed the books back on the shelves and store the computer in her bag knowing that she would have to carried it around only for another day or less. Probably one only extra morning was going to be enough to complete the job. Therefore, she prepare herself to leave the library and head back home.

As she approach the desk to say bye to Matteo, the only interaction he was able to pull up was a "Will you be back tomorrow?" His tone was so neutral that she could not tell if the question was asked out of formality or because he liked the idea of seeing her again. Perhaps, she started to build castle in her mind that had no foundation. True was that he had never made a move on her of any kind, no particular comments or sign of attention of any kind. They were just two adults who had spent a great time together only few nights before just chatting and sharing past experiences. Selin was really hoping that her mind could be able of suppress those silly teenage thoughts and put aside, once and for all, those romantic fantasies.

The next day, the morning went by quickly. By lunchtime Selin had officially ended her work with Bros&Brothers and maybe her career as lawyer. As she pressed the send button, a decade of her life pass in front of her eyes -at the sound of a click. Stretching her arms over the head, she also heard another noise, less intense and emblematic. She heard the sound of her stomach asking for food. Red cheeks, Selin place her hands on her belly in an attempt to cover the noise. It was time to evaluate her alternatives. Usually for lunch she would go to bite something quickly in a bar next door or skipping the lunch or, eventually, going back to her parents home when she felt like having a longer break. Today she would have definitely opt for a family lunch! Her sister Amaia was going to be the chef and her mind cross a heavenly state at the memory of that perfect fit of flavours that only Amaia and her mother were able to magically combine into one perfect harmony. As she collected her staff, Matteo approached her to ask her to lunch together, adding a new and equally attractive alternative to her own list.

Certainly, her silent didn't go unnoticed. Once again her brain found struggle in seeking words. Luckily, Matteo realized that was up to him to continue the conversation.

"I mean, today is a beautiful day. It would be worthwhile to spend it outdoors. Also there is a nice park nearby, and I have prepared enough food for two. So if you like we can have lunch together."

"Oh, of course. Sure! It's just that I thought you could not get away from your desk, not even for lunch."

"You're right. But in the end, I thought: it's your last day in the library. That's a good reason to celebrate! And let's be honest, no one will notice that the library will be closed during the lunch break. Look around you: apart from some student forced by teachers to do research, here there is no one. I'm more than confident I can ward off without problems."

Selin could not help but smiling. In fact, she realized that most of the times she was the only person to go into the library for the whole day. Clearly, going to the library was not a popular hobby for the inhabitants of her home-town.

"Let me finish to collect my things and I am ready."

Matteo had really planned everything. As they got to the park he placed a blanket on the ground where they could sit and share the food. Loads of sandwiches and fruits and sweets came out from his very big lunch box. A fresh bottle of a Spanish rosé wine made that outdoor escape worthy.

Selin wondered if in his head this could be considered a date. If that was the case, she would have been more than happy.

"I'm not a great cook" Matteo felt compelled to add in showing the bunch of sandwiches he had prepared "but I believe to be very good at slicing bread and chop vegetables" he spoke with that shy expression which made him even more fascinating for her eyes.

"It's perfect. I'm glad you thought of me for this picnic. It's an incredible day, the sun is wonderful, the sky is free from any cloud and, wow ... probably I would not have ever noticed all this natural beauty if you hadn't push me out here. It was such a long time I didn't walk in this park. It's so relaxing."

"Well, then I consider myself personally responsible for your reconnect with nature. Anyway, tell me how your work is going?"

"Actually, I'm proud to announce I'm all done! This morning I was able to complete the delivery steps. Furthermore, yesterday I called my boss and told him goodbye. But with the promise that if the conditions change I may return one day in Milan and perhaps open the door to a new cooperation. Say goodbye to my life in Milan was not as simple as I expected: since I returned, Milan has lost its interest and therefore I do not mind having closed that chapter but I have always loved my job and this closure is very bad for me. In short, I told him that, for now, I would have stayed here and, even though I am devoted to my work, the idea to go away again from my family make me nervous. Even more, it destroys me the idea that my father would be on his own once that ... that ..."

"How is your mother?"

"She seems good! There are some times when you look at her, and she's so pale and quiet that you expect her to pass out at any moment. But in general, she is good. She can no longer make physical efforts as before but it is normal, -she is weak. The doctor keeps telling us that we should not be fooled by how well she may looked   because this it may end at any moment, without realizing it."

"And how are you?"

"I am grateful for every day that I am able to spend with my mother. It's amazing! My mother and I have never had a good relationship. But all this has given me the desire to know her as a person and not just as a mother. And what I found was a completely new person. A person that I had no idea existed inside my mother's body. At the same time I discovered a new self. I feel much more positive and less stressed out."

"That's the beauty of living in a smaller and intimate reality. Obviously there are problems but the way of looking at things is totally different. Reality is in the eye of the beholder, in the end. You can have a beautiful day or a horrible day, it all depends on how you choose to live it. And I think that in smaller towns is easier to share a smile rather than being overwhelmed by tension and conflict."

"I like the way you approach life. And maybe this is just what has changed in me, my perspective is different."

"You know, since your birthday party my mother does nothing but talk about you."

"Really? What does she says?"

"She keeps repeating that you promised to visit her. I'm sorry, but I don't know why my mother became obsessed with you. She said you remind her of your mother when she was young. In you she sees her childhood friend. Would you mind to come and visit her in one of the next upcoming days. I think you would make her immensely happy."

"It would make me happy because she promised to talk about my mother: how she was, who she was when she was young -before having her kids. But I'll need a guide. I don't have a car and I don't know your mother's address. And even if I knew where you live, believe me, my sense of direction leaves much to be desired. I don't want to be a burden, but I was already thinking to ask you because I would really like to see her again."

"Do you have something to do in the afternoon? My mother is always home after lunch to do cleaning and watching some program on television. I'm sure she'll be happy to have someone to chat with. With the car will take as only few minutes. If you like, we can even finish the lunch and then go"

"I like the idea."

They ended up spending a few hours in the park to eat and to chat about this and that. At one point Selin could feel the wine beginning to make its effect on her body. She felt her cheeks tinged with a faint reddish and his lips stretched into a uncontrollable smile. Her mind felt more courageous to express herself and so taken by the irrepressible curiosity, Selin surrendered herself and asked him: "I don't want to sound too intrusive, so feel free to don't answer my question, but I have to ask. Several people have mentioned to me about something in your past. About something that's happened to you. There's a lot of gossiping whenever your name is pronounced or whenever you're in the surroundings. I never wanted to dig any further because, in short, it is your private life and it didn't seem fair to me that others speak about you. But I would really like to understand what everyone knows that I don't. How come everyone is talking about you behind your back?" Selin could see his face turning from a perky, cheerful and smiling boy in a dark and lost in himself kind of person.

He did not answer, and when the silence began to be oppressive, Selin felt she had to say something and change the subject.

"Did I tell you that yesterday I went shopping with my sisters and my mother. We bought so many things!" she said with a way too enthusiastic voice.

At least she managed to make Matteo laugh for quite a while. Selin began to feel a sense of discomfort.

Once Matteo was able to stop laughing he said "I'm sorry if I made you feel uncomfortable but you are so cute when you're embarrassed. I want to answer your question, I was just lost in my memories."

He felt like he needed another minute for himself before he was able to speak about that painful memory "I was married once, and in love, completely in love. We had been married for three years when she had an accident and died. Maybe I should have told you before but I really don't like talking about it. Probably because I feel condemned to live with a sense of guilt that haunts me every time I think of her and what happened. And that is because that very morning we had a fight and I still cannot forgive myself for that. We had problems at that time. I wanted to have children: I had a wife, I had a good job (at that time I owned my own business), we possessed our own home. It seemed only natural to also have children. But she would not hear of it. She felt too young, she still wanted to spend all her time hanging out with friends and she wasn't sure she ever wanted to become a mother. And when I realized that she was serious about not wanted to have kids, I felt I lost my balance. I was struggling with myself. I didn't want to leave her because we really loved each other: I was always thinking about her when she wasn't around; my only worry was of how to make her happy; my only need was for us to be together. And she felt the same! Therefore, in the past months when the issue re-emerged, or rather when I tried to open a possibility, a hope among us, we inevitably found ourselves discussing.

And the same happened the morning of the accident. It was horrendous, we said terrible things and, for the first time, at one point she told me she was not even so sure to love me. She said that I loved her too much and she could not compete with my love. She felt suffocated by me and felt as if she had to prove every day her feelings for me. She needed space.

I never suspected in all the years of courtship and marriage that she could ever feel that way. Why she didn't say anything to me before? All my certainties disintegrated right there. We stop talking to each other for the entire day.

Even now, sometimes, I wonder if she really stopped loving me, if she really meant all those things she said. Maybe she was just angry. The fact is that, that same evening, without saying anything to me, she went out with her friends. They went clubbing outside town and they drank a lot. My wife, Nadia, became drunk. Her friends left the pub, at a certain point, and asked her to go with them -that they were calling a cab to go back safe all together. But she didn't want to listen. She didn't want to come back home to me. Nadia stood there drinking while all her friends chose to return to their families. Having fun, for her, had become more important than trying to fix things between us. That night I've tried to call her so many times but no response. I thought she decided to spend the night with one of her friends because of all the tension between us. Truth was, when she finally got to her car, she was so drunk that soon after that car collided straight against a wall. Nadia didn't make it.

When that night, it was almost sunrise, I received a call from the hospital, I felt paralysed. I found it difficult to even breathe. I had to see her covered with wounds, that pale body, lifeless. I felt as if it was me, with my constant insistence, to have caused the accident. Nadia was dead because of me.

Every day since then, I continued to live again in my head the conversation we had that morning. I regretted pushing her to hate me so much that she didn't want to come back home to me.

Soon after I lost my job: I neglected the house, I neglected myself. Just a few months and I was not even able to pay the mortgage. I lost my home, our home, and this only increased that sense of failure that I felt inside me. I failed Nadia and I could not forgive myself for that. I returned to live with my mother.

Slowly I had lost all of my friends who could no longer tolerate the sight of me as a self-destroyed person. My mother was the only one, in that tumult, that stood by me. She was the only one that continued to try to save me from myself. One day she screamed desperate to stop, that the agony was unbearable, that for her I was dead the same night in which Nadia had had the accident. I was dead to her. I was dead inside. And then she told me she had an idea that might saved me.

She told me that life was not always so difficult.

She told me that there was a place where she and I had been happy.

A place where I was a carefree child and she was a woman surrounded by friends and interests. My mother lost her husband, my father, only a few years earlier from a heart attack. I believe this was the reason why she could understand so well the pain I was going through. But unlike me she had been able to be strong and overcome it, or learn to live with it.

The point is that, after my father's death there was not much left for her in that town. She had moved in there in order to follow her husband and without him it made no sense for her to stay.

She staid for me.

But once she realize how all the memory connected to that place were destroying me, she finally took courage and she told me to go back there where we had been happy. Both. Those words somehow stick into my brain and for days it sounded like music in my head. Probably because my mother, for all my life, had done nothing but repeating how happy she was in here that I hoped this town had on me the same power.

Finally, I opened my eyes and realized that there were no more space for me over there. Within three days my mother and I, we packed everything and we moved back here, in our childhood town. After eight months from Nadia's death, we left everything and we started a new life.

That library was the first job I could find and I was very happy because it enabled me to continue my grief in my own time, without the constant stress of having to deal with people and having to provide explanations. At first it was my hiding space, now it is for me the place that gave me my peace. And I am so grateful for it. I think this is one of the reasons why I love working there.

However, I would say this is all!

This is my past that people love so much to talk about."

Selin felt so stupid and selfish. Always so focused on herself and her problems that she had not realized how much weight those shoulders were carrying and how much pain those eyes contained "I'm sorry, I had no idea. I should never have asked you anything. I was a fool. I made you relive that nightmare. I'm really sorry!"

"Don't worry. You know, one of the things I like about you is that, despite living in a small town like this, you are able to lock yourself into your own world and be unaware of everything that happens around you. Somehow you manage not to get carried away by the desire to gossip around -as everyone does here- and it's not easy. However, don't worry about me. It has now been four years and I've had plenty of time to process and accept the situation. I created my balance in this world. However, I must admit that seeing you walk through that door two weeks ago has put a strain on my balance."

"Really?"

He cleared his throat and tried to change the subject "More wine?"

"Yes, thanks."

"You know, Saturday night comes in town a new movie that I really would like to go to see, and I was wondering if you would go there with me."

"I would love to".

They continued to chat for a bit to then head together toward Matteo's car and from there, to his mother's house.

Her house was very, very eclectic and Selin could not help but noticing it aloud. Mrs. Pina smiled as Matteo explained on behalf of the mother "You must know that is now a while that my mother has discovered the passion for travel. Mum makes at least two trips a year in a European town, which are usually short and cheap. And once a year she goes outside the continent for a longer and more intense journey. She has now visit most of Europe and something of the other continents. The problem is that she is not satisfied, as normal people, to buy a magnet or a postcard as a small reminder of the experience ... no! She buys big, literally. Vases, paintings, plants, masks, spices. Mention one crazy thing and I'm sure she has bought it."

Everyone laughed at the story of how Mrs. Pina was spending her time. The most fascinating and interesting thing, among all the junk that occupied that house, was the look of pride for herself, for what she had been able to do with her life, and a large part also directed to her son and the man who over time he had become.

"And this vase, where it comes from?" said Selin pointing to an atypical vase. It had various shades of gold, shaped as two arms that stretched around the entire circumference of the vessel, from top to bottom, where the two hands were touching and the fingers interlaced. It was a fascinating work and Selin could understand the desire of wanting that piece of art in her home in order to enjoy its beauty day after day.

"It is impossible not to notice it, isn't it?" said Mrs. Pina "In fact, is one of the finest pieces of my collection. I bought it in Greece, in Athens four years ago, or maybe a little longer ago. It struck me immediately because it is so different from the Hellenistic tradition and yet retains that part of the tradition that is so strong and felt in that city. I visited quite few cities in Greece and I think that Athens is the most authentic of all, the one still steeped in history and its origins. Look at the base of the pot. Even if all the work is quite modern, there are these two centimetres at the base who are totally immersed in the mythology. You can see representations of battles between gods that are simply astonishing."

Selin had not noticed the base and in light of the new information that work took on even more value.

Ms. Pina continued to speak "I would like to show you something even more beautiful."

They moved into the living room where immediately she could notice a painting that covered the entire length of one of the walls. It was something huge and masterful that attracted everyone attention. "It is a wallpaper that I bought in Turkey when I went there last year. I visited for a week Olüdeniz, a small town in the south of Turkey, in the Fethiye region.

It is a perfect place to relax or even venturing into unforeseen activities. The sea is lovely and walking about twenty minutes west you can find a little corner of paradise they call the Blue Lagoon, where the water is of an intense colour and mountains are all around. My week there passed quickly thanks to the fact that the locals have created so many leisure activities to make you forget about the time going by. Can you believe that one day I even took part in a Jeep Safari? I met the wackiest people. There was this English couple for example. The husband was pretending to be an actor and recited parts of a movie and we had to guess what movie it belonged to. There was also this lovely Turkish homosexual couples where one of the two boys was so happy and full of energy for good part of the journey he did nothing but singing and dancing. We climbed a mountain, walked over a small bridge over a canyon, spread our body with mud in a natural reserve and had tea lying on the floor, along a river.

I then attended a one-day cruise in the surroundings where we were able to see a wonderful giant turtle swimming peacefully in the Aegean Sea. I will never forget that day! But the craziest thing I've done in Olüdeniz was skydiving. It is a very common activity in that area. They pick you up in the morning with a bus from your hotel and take you to the top of the mountain. There is just a short path that needs to be done on foot because cars are not authorized. Then they place all this harness belt around your body and tell you to take three steps and a small jump... and there you are, flying down the mountain above the sea for around twenty minutes before to land on the beach. Believe me, only the thoughts of it makes my legs shake even now. But believe me guys, the adrenaline you feel and that circulates throughout the body is amazing. It is a unique experience and I hope one day you will have the chance to try it out. Certainly Turkey has fascinated me and is one of those places that I wish to explore a bit more.

However, this wallpaper represents the city of Olüdeniz and its beauty!

And I would add that I have been talking no stop since you guys arrived. And I have not even offered a drink. Forgive me but I saw so many beautiful things in the past few years that I could just keep talking about it for hours.

Please, Selin be my guest," said Mrs. Pina while asking Selin to take her place on the couch with herself sitting next to her and Matteo sitting on a chair in front of them. Selin kept staring at a very particular centrepiece placed on the table next to them and wondered what was the story behind that.

"This house has so much to tell and I can only imagine how precious it has been to live all this wonderful experience and have a chance to share it. I envy you!" Selin could not refrain herself from expressing "I've been a few times to Barcelona to visit my brother Stefano and once in London to see the youngest of the family, Arianna. But it is nothing compared to the experiences that you have collected over the years. This house seems to have a soul, the soul of a traveller. I always liked the idea of travelling a bit myself and explore the world but I always got caught a bit too much in my job and at the end I never went anywhere."

"Honey I can only give you one advice. And my advise is, if you want to do something do it, do not postpone. Life is long but it is shorter than it seems." answered Pina and turning to Matteo "Matteo dear, do me a favour and go to prepare some tea. Also bring the cookies that are on the top shelf in the kitchen. Too much talk makes me hungry," she said, smiling.

Turning back toward Selin "dear, how do you like your tea? I have all kinds, name one and I'm sure I have it."

"I like green tea if it's not too much trouble"

"And green tea is. Matteo, green tea for Selin and the lemon and ginger for me. Thanks."

"No problem, mum," said Matteo headed for the kitchen.

Mrs. Pina put her hand on Selin's one as soon as Matteo left the room. Looking deeply in her eyes said "The truth, young girl, is that after my husband died, now many years ago, I felt lost and alone. Travel has been my way to channel my grief into something that would give me strength, energy and that would surprise and amuse me at the same time. Travelling has been my lifeline during the most difficult years of my life. Anyway, I'm pretty sure you did not come all this way to listen to my travel stories, right?"

"Actually I think I could listen to talk about your travels for days. The way you are telling those stories it is so exciting that it makes me want to learn more and I promise to return very soon to hear some other adventure. But if it's fine for you, for today I'd like to get to know my mother a little more. I'd like to know who was my mother as a young girl, when she went out with her friends, when she went to school and so on."

"Well, let's see. What to say! Your mother has always possessed a very sociable personality. She always loved to have many friends, so many people to talk too. And she's always been a good listener, and this made her very popular. We all knew we could go to her and talk about any thing without hesitation or fear of being judged. Your mother and I were neighbours. Our doors were facing one another. Our mothers were friendly with each other but they had a pure neighbourhood relationship. During the elementary school, we found ourselves in the same class and as we started to talk a bit more between us we ended up growing up to do homework together sometimes at my house, sometimes at her house. We did together also middle school. When we turn fourteen, we both chose to attend high school here in the village, a little because your mother had the need to stay close to her brother's school and a little because we liked to immerse ourselves in reading books that can transport us elsewhere with the mind, -therefore we didn't mind if our body stayed in town. Sometimes, we would decide to ditch school and we would walked down the streets of the old town, near the castle, exploring the streets, caves, churches, debating our future, our dreams, our reality. Then I started to date one of our classmate who came from another small village nearby, while your mother met a boy during one of our outings, your dad, and this slowly led to separate our roads for a little while."

"How did my parents met? When we tried to ask my mother she's always so vague about it."

"If I remember correctly we were seventeen and your mother and I were heading to the park. We were walking the streets when right next to your mother fell an iron pipe from a scaffold attached to a house under construction. You can not imagine the scare that we took. A boy began immediately to descend from the scaffolding to come to check if we were okay. It looked like a monkey for the agility with which jumped from side to side. He apologized a hundred times, he admitted that it was all his fault, that the pipe had slipped from his hands as he tried to pass it to a colleague. Will have had twenty years at the time and he gave the impression of a very shy and introverted guy. Your mother told him not to worry, that we were fine. She asked him his name and left. From the day after your mother always wanted to do that road every time we had to go to the park. And every time we passed next to the construction site your mum would scream 'hello Claudio' with her cheerful and opened smile of those who had a big crush. And he blushed every time. One day, while walking there your mother saw that Claudio was taking a break with his colleagues, and ran to meet him, stunning him with her chatting. Even today the only memory makes me laugh so hard. But her stubbornness helped Claudio to unlock and open up a bit more.

They went on for a couple of months, every time your mother passed by, Claudio would take his break and they would talk for half an hour. When your father one day said that their work was over, your mother, as if nothing, told him 'well, it means that now you have to invite me out, I would say this Friday night is perfect for a date'.

So, the following week they had their first date, the two of them, alone. Immediately they became a couple and when your mother turned eighteen they got married. Your father adored her, and for what I saw at the party, things have not changed after almost forty years of marriage but, if possible, are even more intense now than they were then."

"Wow, it's hard to think my mother be so fearless with the boys" Selin said between laughs.

"My dear, the surprising thing is that your mother was not fearless at all. I mean, she certainly was a person who loved to chat, but flirt?!? this was a game she could not play at all. In some way, and a little before their wedding she clearly told me so, from the first moment she saw him, she knew that he would become an important part of her life."

"Really? And how she was able to figure it out?"

"I have no clue. I can tell you that your mother always knew what she wanted. She wanted a family, children, a house and I can only imagine that your father wanted the same things."

"Were you there when we were born or had you already changed the city?"

"I was there when your eldest sister was born and at that time your mother was the happiest person in the world. But two years later when she announced to be pregnant again, I was packing up to relocate to another town and I myself was pregnant with Matteo, very close to give birth. But as I told you already at the party, for the first few years we were able to keep in touch. Seeing at least a couple of times a year. Letting you two guys playing together. Believe me, your mother always had so many good things to tell me about you. Every time she came to visit me she would tell me about you and your success. From having learned to walk, to a good grade in school, to having uttered your first word. Whatever you did for her it was special. She's always been very proud of you. When you decided to move so far away, your mother found it difficult to accept it. I think she had a problem with letting you go.

With your two youngest siblings it was simpler because she knew what was happening but you were her first.

I mean, the first to decide that didn't want to spend her life in her home town. The first to decide that life wasn't enough as it was.

And for her it was personal. After having loved so much your daughter, understand that for her you are not enough hurts a lot. Believe me! For quite a while she was mad at you even though she tried to support your choices. And it was very hard for her to understand and accept them. The pride in your success was not lacking: when you graduate into law school the whole town knew about it. She could not restrain herself. On the other hand, she didn't know any more how to communicate with you. Suddenly you two were speaking different languages and she was not able to adapt."

"Truth is, that I have made it very difficult for her to talk to me. For years I have created an impenetrable wall for my mother and the rest of the family."

"Honey, you were just a teenager girl and there is no teenager who doesn't build a wall against their parents. I speak from personal experience." She said, smiling toward Matteo. "Unfortunately for you, your mother had as first daughter Amaia that was very easy to handle because they were exactly alike. They wanted the same things out of life. This create in her mind the illusion that all kids must be the same. You broke that illusion." she added in between laughs. Then returning serious "but that doesn't mean she loved you any less."

"I know, I know."

"More tea, dear?"

"No no thank you. In fact I think I abused too much of your kindness. It is so nice to chat with you that I have completely lost the notion of time. Now I understand by whom your son has taken this quality."

Everyone smiled.

"I have to go," said Selin, rising from the couch.

"Just a moment. I've got something for your mother."

Mrs. Pina walked away in the direction of the kitchen.

She reappear a couple of minutes later with a very colourful gift bag. It is a pack of coffee. A few months ago I went to Venezuela and found this shop that sold various kinds of coffee all with spectacular aromas. And I thought of your mother. She loves coffee, and I wanted her to try a whole new scent. I'm sure she'll like it a lot."

"It will be done. Thanks so much for this wonderful day. It will be hard to forget." They hugged each other and said goodbye.

Matteo walked her to the door and said goodbye with a promise to meet again on Saturday night to go to the movies.

The following days went by fast. Selin and her siblings were always around their mother always inventing new things to do together or simply enjoying a coffee.

Actually, the two youngest one had fun pulling out Matteo's name whenever they could. Simply for the fun of seeing her blush.

And their mother who teased them up and begged them to let their big sister alone. Truth was, it was all her fault. She had given Mrs. Pina's gift for her mother when everyone was present. It turned out to be a mistake of catastrophic proportions. From that moment on her siblings did nothing but teasing with hallucinatory as embarrassing theories on what could it have happened between the two of them in Matteo's house -not paying much attention to the detail of his mother being present. Even worse, she had told them of their little picnic in the park.

She didn't want to keep secrets from her family but consequently the youngest of the house could not help but have fun at her expenses.

But apart from the inevitable blush that tinged her cheeks she could not deny to find cute the way they were making fun of her.

Saturday evening arrived quickly and it was like be in a fairy tale. Mostly she felt like Cinderella, with her little siblings who were playing the role of the mice trying choosing for her the most suitable outfit for the evening. Their first choice fell on a mini red dress that clung her body in a provocative manner without leaving much to the imagination.

"If you go out with that dress, I believe we will not see you for a week or so. Do you know what I mean?" said Stefano laughing.

She immediately abolished the choice, even though Arianna seemed enthusiastic about it. And it made Selin wondered why her baby sister had such an outfit at her disposal. The second choice fell on a candy pink dress that also had a hat in a British royals' style.

Selin comment stupefied "no way! I really have to ask you why the hell these clothes are in your closet. No one would ever dare to use them in real life."

"My dear big sister, may I remind you that sometimes I take part in fashion shows or do photo shoots for British magazines. And, you know how it works! If you are nice, sometimes they leave you the clothes which you have posed with as a souvenir of the experience. And personally I find them cute, at least much more interesting than your boring office clothes." Arianna replied.

"Okay, let's put the record straight, I love my boring office clothes and with them I feel more at ease. So if you want to help, find me something that doesn't make me feel a clown or a very cheap escort."

With a grimace of disapproval Arianna put in the closet yet another dress chosen by her she was aware Selin would not give approval to and began to look for a more sober kind of outfit.

After a bit of searching she pulled out one exclaiming "this is certainly not my first choice when it comes to make a man fall at your feet, but a boring person like you could consider it a cute outfit." This time Arianna had guessed right.

She pulled out a bright blue dress that reached to the knee with a not too excessive side split. Two thin straps connected the front of the dress to the back with a soft stitching on the breast, to then wrap tight around the waist and the hips. Beige high-heeled shoes and two earrings of the same colour give the final touch to her evening look.

Thinking that the hard part was over, she had to change her mind when her brother began to give her advice on sex: on what a men would enjoy been done to them on a first date and that would help her to get a second date. Since her begging him to stop did not lead anywhere, Selin ended quickly to get ready and decided to go and wait for Matteo directly outside the house, at the door. Anyway, few minutes longer and he would have arrived.

When Matteo arrived he was surprised to find her already out of the house, leaning against the door with her eyes lost looking up at the sky.

"Selin hey, are you okay? Has something happened?"

"Hey hello, no it's all right, don't worry. I was just hiding from my siblings. Sometimes it's hard to have anything to do with them: they have too much energy and a few limitations."

Meanwhile, Matteo was out of the car and had accompanied her on the other side by opening the door like a perfect gentleman. Once he returned to the driver seat, exclaimed "it must be nice to have brothers. I've always been an only child but I had many friends with brothers and their relationships were always close. They could argue constantly and being at the some time always so protective with each other. I guess it's the same thing among you and your siblings."

"I have so many siblings and indeed sometimes can be stifling, never having spaces for yourself. But I would not change it for anything in the world. Wherever you are, whatever it happens to you, if you have siblings you know that you'll never be alone. You know you'll always have someone to support you no matter what happens. Somebody who will fight at your side and that will love you unconditionally for the rest of your life. But on the other hand, they do not know the concept of privacy and is always very noisy as I told you already last time. Never a moment of peace. This is what means having siblings."

They chatted pleasantly all the way to the cinema. It was immediately clear that, with him, came really natural to talk about anything and there never were awkward silences. The cinema was practically deserted and the screen broadcasting one of those old comic films in black and white. Apparently Matteo had recently discovered to be a big fan and at least once a month was in this art cinema to rediscover the classics in black and white. Matteo had already seen the movie a few times and Selin could not define herself a fans of the genre: simply was hard to see the humour into it. Often it was not clear what the characters were laughing about. She sensed that there had to be some comic joke but she couldn't share the laugh. With this background, the two of them, after a few minutes, decided not to care too much about the plot. Instead they just kept talking and talking and, soon, their fingers lightly touched. Matteo continued to play with her hand all evening, gently, moving his fingertips on the back of her hand and then drawing little circles on it. By doing so her whole body began to vibrate. She was completely and inevitably lost in him, in his dark eyes, in his strong jaws, in his well designed lips, in his thick neck and his silky hair: everything about him spoke to her.

His body was a continuous communication. She did not even notice the exact moment when they began to kiss as they felt for some time to be one with each other. That contact between their lips was the most delicate and sweet thing that had ever happened. It was as if their lips wedge in perfectly; as if they were built to be one in the infinite world. They continued kissing. Not only for that night but for a long, long time yet to come.

CHAPTER X

"I have a proposal to make" it was about a month after the party. In the meantime her siblings had returned to their respective cities as their duties as a student and bar's owner lured them out of the Country. Amaia, taking advantage of the extended time the children spend in school, was always having lunch at their parents' home. And Selin had started the renovation of her new flat which was going to take a few more months. For her that was okay because she wanted to enjoy as much as possible the familiar atmosphere of mutual acceptance and love that Selin with difficulty had been able to reconstruct. It had not been easy, but the hard shell built in the past it had finally crumbled. She had finally learned to get excited and to express those emotions appropriately -no need to hide behind unnecessary barricades. That day began in the same way: breakfast together, his father going to do some work in the countryside; Selin helping her mum with the cleaning; going out food-shopping together; passing by her new flat to oversee the work and, while the mother returned home and began to prepare for lunch, she would go by the library to spend some time with Matteo.

While everyone was getting ready to give a first bite to their plate of pasta Selin expressed what was going through her mind since a while now, "I have a proposal to make. I know it sounds crazy but let me talk." All eyes fixed on her.

"I am deeply convinced that we all deserve a holiday. The point is that I am forced to go back to Milan because I have to clean up my apartment. I got tired of washing my stuff every other day because here I don't have clothes to wear except those of the high school which I am ashamed of. And if I think that in Milan I have two whole wardrobe completely full I feel even more ridiculous. And honestly I'm paying the rent of a house of which I am aware to never use again in my life. That honestly made me think I could do a more profitable use of that money. Okay, I am not broke but not even rich enough to throw my earnings to the wind. Now, I could go back to Milan alone or I might enjoy your company. I know that Milan may not be your kind of city so the plan is to spend only two days in that city, and then move to London ..."

"What? No dear! You know we can not travel." Interrupted her mother tense.

"Mum, let me finish what I have to say and only then you can express your opinion. My program is not over yet. I was saying, you guys go to London while I still hold back one day in Milan to finish the various packagings and load everything on the transport truck and then join you in London. I thought we could stay there for four days since it is a very big city and then move to Barcelona where we will have a fantastic time and we could also relax on the beach. Then we can take a direct flight back to Bari and back to our dear Bernalda. Now, mum, you can comment" concluded Selin smiling and with obvious pride taken in her idea.

"Honey you are very kind, but going to disturb your siblings while working and studying it seems not the case and you know that your father and I are not used to travel, let alone outside Italy. And who has ever taken a plane in its entire life? Definitely not us. We would get lost inside the airport." She objected hesitant.

"I would take you to the airport so you guys will definitely not getting lost. Once past the gate Amaia will take care of you. She has already travelled by plane and she will lead you and be with you for any need you may have. Arianna will then come and pick you up from the airport and escort you to the hotel and the same will be done in Barcelona. I have already talked to both my siblings and they are both really excited that finally you are going to visit them."

"I'm not sure."

"Mum, you told me a few weeks ago that one of the things that you felt sorry about it was that you never had the chance to see an exhibition of Arianna or see Stefano's bar and the success he is having. Believe me, your child in employer version is a completely new experience that you will not want to lose. And until now, the two of you, had never the chance to travel and enjoy life either because you have been paying our study at uni or because the fear of the unknown took over. The fact is that your children want you to go and visit them and they want to show with pride the cities where they are rediscovering themselves and in which they are experiencing some wonderful adventures."

"And what about Matteo? you have just started dating, and you want to go away for ten days?" replied stubborn her mother.

"It is going to be only nine days and not ten, mum. And honestly Matteo supports me and my ideas fully. Indeed, he hopes we will enjoy the journey as much as possible."

"And you Amaia, would you leave your kids alone for so long?" try to say her mother noticing that with Selin she was fighting a battle she could not win.

"My husband and my sister in law will take care of them. Mum, I honestly believe that Selin had a fantastic idea, and as soon as she shared this project with me she had me completely on her side. You deserve this holiday -we deserve this holiday! I understand this is something completely new to you but in this family we can no longer postpone the life. We must seize every opportunity for happiness in the moment that is given to us." Said Amaia.

"You have other comments?" Quipped Selin.

"Given that you've thought of everything, tell me who will take care of your father's countryside and who will oversee the workmen in your new apartment? And even more, if you send a moving van from Milan who will be here waiting for downloading? If you answer these questions I surrender" her mother said with a shy smile that was beginning to appear on her lips.

"I went to talk to the uncles and they will take care of both the countryside that the apartment and Stella will take care of the moving van. She has already a spare key. And I already informed the moving guy that they will need to call Stella as soon as they get in town so Stella will have the time to come home and with her boyfriend will take care of downloading the whole thing in the garage."

"Have you already contacted the moving company? Do you already know when to leave for Milan?"

"Mum there's just one thing I haven't told you yet. I have already booked the whole trip for all of us. We depart on Sunday."

"What?" Said the father and mother in unison.

"My lovely parents, you have three days to prepare your bags and surrender yourself to have the nine best days of your life. Enjoy your meal." Selin finally said starting to eat that now a bit cold plate of pasta with a sense of joy that pervaded her all over.

At ten in the evening of that very Sunday they were all at the train station ready to face the first part of their new adventure. Selin had thought that a first quiet overnight trip, would have been the least traumatic choice for her parents. Apparently, her parents were really ready for anything: they were loaded with not only two hand luggage but also two extra big luggages. It seemed like her mother had planned to go from the equator to the pole north and forth carrying with them every type of imaginable clothing. Furthermore, she had also brought tons of food that ranged from oranges, friselle, zucchini, fresh olive oil made by their father and so on. Her mother had confused the city with a long and desolate deserts. She had tried several times to explain to her that they were going to visit some of the greatest metropolises of Europe which had a lot of food choice to offer but those were her mum's conditions to get into that train. Fortunately Amaia was much more reasonable and one luggage was all she needed. Selin, from her side, she didn't need to bring anything at all but her purse. All of her clothes were in her apartment in Milan and she was going to organize her luggage while in there. At least, in this way she was able to help her parents in transporting those "houses on wheels" they had prepared for themselves.

There was still a ten minutes waiting time before their train arrived, when Selin heard someone calling her name. It was a cheerful and young male voice coming from her back which she immediately recognized it as belonging to Davide -the boy she had met the night she had discover about her mother sickness. They had not crossed each other path since the morning she had left him asleep on that couch. Although she was well aware that they lived in the same town and that sooner or later their paths would cross again. As soon as she turned, she could feel his arms wrap her waist in a warm and friendly hug as she could feel the questioning eyes on her parents and sister pressing on the back of her head.

"Hi Selin, how you're doing?"

"Davide, what a surprise! I'm fine, thanks. What about you?"

"Great. Gee is a lifetime we do not see each other. That morning you left without even leave me your phone number. I did not know how to contact you. Damn, that night was incredible. You were amazing." And he hug her again.

Selin could feel her cheeks on fire and her sister waiting with a flood of questions ready to inundate while standing next to her just to make sure she would not miss a bit of that conversation. Fortunately her parents had left discreetly to allow them a bit of space.

"Emmmmh, thank you! But what are you doing here at the station? Are you leaving?" ask Selin trying to change subject.

"No, not me. I'm here with my girlfriend, Francesca," and so saying a beautiful girl, very thin and very young materialized beside him, wrapping her arm around his shoulder.

"Love, this is Selin, I told you about her" on his lips always that big smile while Selin felt like melting down from the embarrassment of the entire situation. She could not refrain herself from asking how long they were together and when the answer given was five years, the embarrassment on her face was crystal clear.

"But it's all cool, I will never cheat on my girl. It's just that time to time we feel the need to split up and whatever happens when we are not together it doesn't count. Am I right, sweet pie?"

"All is cool" Francesca said as she continued to chew her chewing gum in a very unglamorous way "Babe, we got to go to my track. In a few minutes my train will be here."

"Of course, honey. Selin, I wanted so much to see you to tell you what's been between us helped me to write a song and Francesca says that rocks. You've inspired me" and after one last final hug, he add "Francesca will obviously not be happy if we see each other again, and I don't want to upset her. She's scary when she gets angry. She throws staff at me, sometimes very heavy one's. But even though I can not see you any more I wanted to thank you. You are fantastic. Bye bye." Said so, he ran toward his girlfriend and away from her.

Despite everything, Selin could not suppress a smile. That guy had an incredible energy and somehow had gifted her with a bit of that energy. She had to admit that since she had learned to let herself go with him, she had also learned to live her life by taking a few more risks without fear. Ultimately, they had inspired each other.

The announcement of their train approaching startled Selin from her thoughts. She turned on herself and her sister's angry face made her smile disappear.

"Are you betraying Matteo?" asked Amaia without holding herself back.

"What? No, no, no, no, no. Are you kidding? I would never betray Matteo. You know how crazy I am about him. I didn't even know Matteo when all of this happen, when all the Davide's thing was on."

"You got to tell me how in hell you know that guy because last I check you have no friends in town -no that young anyway."

"Instead of stay here out chatting we better start to organize our luggages on the train before our exiting journey got ruined by a boy."

"It does not end here." Said seriously Amaia while grabbing on of her parents big luggage and with effort start to loading it onto the train.

Selin smiled knowing that somehow she had win her sister back. It had not been easy but her continues stubbornness opened a passage between the two sisters. She knew now that Amaia had started to forgive her for having forgotten to have a big sister in previous years.

That night, as the train carried them into a new world for her family, and their parents were fast asleep, the two sisters share confidences as happened to them when they were fifteen. Selin told her all about herself, the herself of the past few months, the internal changes that she had faced and how scare she was to go back to live the way she had lived for so long. She told her about the night with Davide in which she had took refuge to hide from the truth, and how she realized that in her life she had done nothing but hide: hide behind her work, behind Milan, behind any thing just to avoid having to ask herself who she was. She told her to be really happy to have found her sister and once again apologized for having taken her for granted. But this time Amaia forgave her and while the train kept running and the sisters kept chatting the sun rose on the horizon.

The two days in Milan rapid flew between mornings spent been tourists and the afternoons spent to pack up Selin's past in several boxes. At night she would spoiled them by going out to dinner in downtown's restaurant. They visited the cathedral of the city -this symbolic monument of Milan-; the Sforzesco Castle -one of the largest castles in Europe-; the Scala theatre, one of the most famous theatre in the world, with its neoclassical façade, that for over two hundred years had hosted internationally recognized artists. And of course they visited the Galleria Vittorio Emanuele II, the covered walkway that connects Corso Vittorio Emanuele II with Piazza Beccaria famous as fashionable place and a meeting point for musicians thanks to three cinemas and two theatres located in the proximity. As she expected, her parents did not prove to be particularly excited about that city that had hosted her for so many years. It was a vibrant city: you could only love her or hate her, there was no room for shades of grey. And the approach of summer with its high temperatures, it meant   sultriness in big cities like Milan that made it in their eyes even less hospitable. However, she was surprised when her mother asked her "my dear, your father and I have embarked on this journey to understand the life that our children are living and not for sightseeing. We would be much happier if we could understand a little better your life here in Milan. If possible we would like to visit the place where you worked for so long."
It was embarrassing to have to call Gabriele, her former employer to ask if a former employee could bring her parents to visit her former workplace. And when she found the courage to dial the number and heard Gabriele saying "come around two o'clock that I have one hour to spare and we could all go to eat at Marco's" convinced her that she had found and lost the best boss anyone could ever wish for.
Standing in front of that imposing building with the inscription Bros & Brothers that stood out above the front door, was for Selin a pushed back to that last day when she run away from that very door expecting to be back after only a couple of days. Her old self would have never believed that that was the last time she would have come back to that firm as employee. A deep breath, and together they explored that part of her life that no one had ever access before. It was comforting and at the same time made her nostalgic to find that nothing had changed, that the energy of the place was still intact. Phones

ringing constantly, people running from side to side, desperate customers screaming. For her parents it was difficult to understand why she loved that daily madness, but her devotion to that place had always been intact and she still felt that devotion inside her even if she was no longer part of that team.

Gabriele saw her approaching from distance, and with open arms welcomed her and her entire family. He hugged immediately Selin's mother. A long, strong hug "Mrs Giovanna, you cannot believe how sorry I am. I can not even imagine what you are facing. But you must know that you had given birth to one of the most talented and fearless civil lawyers who's ever crossed my path. You can only be proud of her."

"I am, believe me." Replied her mother convinced.

"My dear Selin, have you already shown them your old office?" And after a positive nod of her head he said, "Good, because I am famishing."

So saying they headed to Marco's, a small pizzeria nearby where all of the lawyer from the firm enjoyed a little distraction between one case and the other.

But this time Selin, after crossing that front door, she turned on her feet in order to give a last goodbye to that place that held so many beautiful memories. As usual Gabriele entertained her parents with continuous chatter, he was a great orator and his parents were completely charmed by him. This was his technique. You could say that he had a habit of stun people with his eloquence. But it was always a pleasure to listen to that warm voice spreading into the air. They talked about Selin, about who she was when only twenty-four she appeared in his firm. That tiny girl with a great desire to learn and ready to challenge the world. They also talked about the type of cases his firm usually dealt with and what kind of lawyer Selin was, how she tackled her client list.

All the family was very surprised when Gabriele finally proposed to go to see a real case, in a real court with real lawyers in action. Despite the surprise, her mother was very excited and was the first one to accept the offer. Now totally conquered, her mother soon forgot to have a husband and took Gabriele by the arm and went with him up to the courthouse stairs listening spellbound explanations he provided of the structure, its history and the most dangerous criminals who crossed that threshold. Selin, Amaia and their father a few meters behind commented laughing at the joyful expressions of their mother who had never shown so much interest in the subjects of history and architecture or legislature for what it was worth. Inside the court they had to separate themselves as Gabriele was due to meet his client and prepare himself to argue his case while they took place inside the courtroom.

The mother barely restrained applauses when she saw Gabriele entering the courtroom and did nothing but shake her head whenever he spoke. All of a sudden, she turned toward Selin asking softly "Selin, why did you leave your job? Are you crazy? Your boss is so fascinating."

All laughed and Selin now with tears in her eyes said, "I remember someone told me that there is not only the job in life, that there are much more important things which we should focus on. And I just listened to that advice."

"Now listen to this other advice instead: never take seriously a mother's advice. I was crazy. Who would not want to work with a man like that, put criminals in jail, talk in front of a judge about justice."

"Mum, I love my job and perhaps I will never get to work with Gabriele ever again but I will return to fight the criminals among classrooms court. Or rather resolve quarrels between neighbours in court," she added as her sister and her father continued to laugh. "But, most of all, I'm glad to know you approve my career choice."

At the end of the debate, the family quickly saluted Gabriele, who needed to stay there again to talk to his client and, after further intense hugs between him and her mother, they went back to Selin's apartment where they ordered some take-away food, packed up more of Selin's staff and went to bed early because the next morning was waiting for them another day of travel.

They had to get up early and go to the airport where they enjoyed a breakfast together before her parents and her sister crossed the gate and Selin made a quick return to her apartment where she was well aware she had half a day to pack up the rest of her stuff and load them on the transport trucks that would arrive that very evening. And the very next day, returned the keys of her apartment and get ready to join again her family for the second part of that journey which was going to take her to London.

Selin had to make a race against time to be able to pack up eleven years of her life in a little over a half of a day. Once in her bedroom she realized that for the first time in weeks she was again alone, really alone and far away from her family. That last month fell on her like if two planes had collided.

From the radio came the notes of a past music, almost forgotten. A sound barely audible but decidedly nostalgic, with a typical bitter taste of an era never lived but dreamed and yearned.

In that room seemingly everything communicated regularity, normality. From the few pictures hanging on those walls the colours a bit timid, almost intimidated to dare, from showing too much security: as if the swagger was abolished. Everywhere it reigned a neutral beige.

... And a newspaper, carelessly open on an unmade bed. Among those pages, various news were fighting for attention: there had been some major competition where someone won and someone else was accepting the defeat sportingly; images reported that there was clearly good weather all week, but as a veiled threat, the weekend seemed to be covered with clouds; and ... The inevitable horoscope, there it was to give false hopes to believers in need "love will come, your life will change, and the sun will shine forever higher in the sky .... for you, only for you, who read and believe in me."

And on that bed her. Sitting there, legs crossed, arms dangling, and a lost look in an unreal dimension. A large bed, a large room, a thin environment and a single person, there in the centre of everything.

Selin could not help but think of how quickly and drastically her life had changed. The person she had been, and the various people she had turn into in those past few months -and how she got to understand and accept the person who she now was. It had been a difficult journey that had turned her into a more peaceful person who had learned to come to terms with herself and to accept herself. A person who knew love and knew how to love, who finally knew how to communicate with people who loved her without hurt anyone. She had finally knocked down that wall of anger and fear that accompanied her for so long and for that she could only say thank you to her mother. Thank you for forcing her to participate to that dinner, thank you for giving her a deadline on her own life and having forced her hand, thank you for opening that window about her past and her weakness as a woman, thank you for having loved her even when she could not return her affection, thank you for having accepted whoever she had been and whoever she was now, thank you for being alive and giving her the opportunity to say thank you. The sound of the phone woke her up from her own thoughts. It was Arianna who sent her a picture of her parents staring enchanted London Eye. The heart sank to the awareness of how many people in her life loved her and how she had been blind in those years not to realize it. And just at that moment also came a message from Matteo "I hope it's not too hard to say goodbye to Milan. This library is too quiet without you. I miss you." Selin still had an hour to pack a duvet and hundreds of boxes to be sealed. She sets her nostalgic thoughts aside and went back in action with the new life that ran through her body and soul and that she liked so much.

On arrival in London, she joined her family in Camden Town, intent on enjoying a lunch in the centre of London's multiculturalism. Her sister Arianna threw her arms around her as soon as she saw her, "Oh my gosh, you've got such a brilliant idea in organizing this trip. Mum and dad are enjoying it very much. Are you hungry?"

"I'm starving!"

"Perfect because after eating I want to take you all to a special place."

"I cannot wait." And when Selin sat down at the table, "hey mum, dad, how it was flying for the first time?"

"It's amazing how those little boxes can keep flying." Replied the father who clearly had had problems in adapting to the aircraft.

"Shut up Carlo! It was just great, we also drank a glass of wine and ate some sandwiches and it was amazing to see the earth from so far away. Think that we walked right into the clouds." replied Giovanna.

"And what have you visited so far?"

"Yesterday we made the rounds on the boat and we went across the Thames from Westminster to Greenwich. We have seen the meridian line and made the picture where it says Italy, look."

"I see you've already seen quite a few things" said Selin smiling.

"Oh honey, I hope you don't mind. We have said that we should wait for you to go sightseeing but Arianna said you would be okay with that."

"Yes Mum, Arianna is right. I already visit this city a couple of times and I had time to do the tourist things. Did you like what you've seen so far?"

"Oh sure. This city is incredible. I must say that I don't like the escalators very much, they move to fast and here it seems like people can not really do without it, but what we have seen is really nice. And you know there are plenty of Italian restaurants? So every time Arianna has homesickness she can go to one of those restaurants. And you cannot imagine how many Italians are out there! But tell me, dear all right with the moving out?"

Selin was glad to see her mother so excited. Finally she was taking that vacation in the way her children hoped: she was curious and passionate. "Yes, yes mum. Everything went just fine. I managed to pack everything up and send all the boxes down to the village. I have already contacted Stella, she will do the rest."

They finished eating by listening to her mother talking exultant about everything that had happened so far. She was like a little girl with wide-enchantment on those eyes as she was discovering new things "And you know that the British say also 'ciao', the same way we say it? Arianna told me."

They walked a little on the streets of Camden by visiting the market and Camden Lock and commenting on every odd sculpture protruding from the walls of the buildings and then get back on the subway not without complaints from her mother on the escalators that were everywhere.

Arianna did not want to tell anyone where they were heading until they would not be there. By underground they arrived to Charing Cross. Their parents were once again shocked by the many faces of London. Every time they came out of the underground was a completely new city waiting for them. It was amazing how there could be so many souls in one place. They walked for a few minutes until Arianna stopped near a glass door on which there was printed in white letter '*temporary exhibition: new generation at work!*'

"Remember I told you that an art gallery had agreed to have some of my paintings on display for six months?" Arianna said.

"Oh you're referring to the two photos?" Amaia said.

"No, that's another show and we will visit it tomorrow. Here are some of my paintings and I hope you enjoy them. After you, guys!"

Amaia was the first to go, followed by their parents, then it was the turn of Selin and Arianna closed the row. The gallery was divided into various sectors, each representing a different theme: animals, universe, sexuality, urban world, technology, and then there was hers. The ward where Arianna had had a chance to exhibit her paintings. The theme was family! They were all amazed to observe themselves once again on canvas but this time they were not simple faces represented on canvas as the one that Amaia made for Selin's birthday. This time they were in their daily lives. The first represented them all around the fireplace listening to their mother intent on talking while their father was asleep in the chair beside it. The next represented her mother intent on making coffee while, with her face turned toward the table behind her. the rest of the family was engaged on having breakfast. In the third painting, Amaia personified a history school teacher and in front of her a bunch of children, or better mini-them, including the grand-kids and the uncles and themselves. They all huddle behind that little school desk with their father who was scratching his head clearly confused, their brother who was looking out the window to a young woman in the garden, Selin with glasses all serious intent to study, Arianna was intent on drawing on the book and her mother who drank her coffee after all. There were six of this paintings in total representing their lives: There was a fourth that represented Selin in the middle of a courtroom with his mother as a judge, his brother at the bar, Amaia as the counterpart and Arianna and her father in the audience. In the fifth, they were in Barcelona, in their brother's bar all sit at the counter side by side while their brother was pouring drinks. And the last painting resumed them in the countryside each intent on collecting something different: their father had a hoe in his hand ready to hit the ground; Arianna and Stefano were intent on eating the grapes directly from the plant; Amaia and Selin were instead around a tree intent to pick oranges and place it into a container nearby while their mother was arranging food on a table in the middle of the painting. The most wonderful part of all those painting was to found written on each of them, in different part of the painting, the words *together forever*. Their mother, deeply moved she burst into tears and put her hands up to cover her eyes. Arianna ran to hug her and whispered in her ear, "Mum, you will live forever!"

The visitors looked curiously at them trying to figure out what was going on until they were picking the similarity between the faces in the paintings and the faces of the real people: her family. Their mother needed a few minutes to compose herself but no one convinced her to leave the art gallery until it was closing time. There was a bench in the middle of that wing, and their parents sat there with their faces turned toward the canvas intent on observing every little detail. And for the two days that were still missing her mother wanted to return every day in that gallery and sit for an hour to observe the paintings. Despite the complaints of others about missing out on others attractions, she was peremptory. They had to go back to that art gallery every day. Arianna forward to her mother phone photos that she had made of all the paintings so that her mother could keep looking at them also when they returned home. The day after Arianna made them also visit the photo exhibition called *details* in which the curator had agreed to produce two of his photographs representing one eye and one drop so that the mother could understand and accept the true passion for photography of her daughter. And her mother understood and accepted her and she actually could not verbalize the enormous pride in all the work and dedication that she had always put in living her life. But they didn't forget to be also tourists and the next morning they went to see Buckingham Palace and the greeting to the Queen to move then to Regents Park and appreciate the beauty of the garden guarded inside, they walked through the streets of Oxford Street and its countless shops and then move to Piccadilly Circus to buy magnets for uncles and friends.

Their holiday in London ended a few days later between general hugs. Unfortunately Arianna could not join them in the last part of their journey. School and work forced her to stay in the area. "Mum, it made me really happy to see you here in the city where I live. I would never have imagined that one day I could hug my parents here in London. I am so so happy!" Arianna told them while waiting for the bus that would take them to the airport.

"My love, to have been able to be part of your life even if only for four days has made me the happiest mother in the world and we are the proudest parents to be found anywhere around. You can not even imagine what a big gift you have given me. I will continue to look at your paintings in every day that I will be given to live." And with one last hug they said goodbye to London while the city of Barcelona gave them welcome. Both her parents immediately fell in love with that city so full of sun, light, sea and life. Some parts of the city reminded him of their own town. They worshipped the Ramblas and all those street artists who were an integral part of it. They fell madly in love with Parc Güell and the multitude of colours that communicated them great joy and zest for life. They let themselves be overwhelmed by the beauty of the Sagrada Familia and its history... But the part of the city that stole their hearts was the magic fountain of Montjuic, a wonderful park that embrace this huge fountain that offered a unique show in its beauty, with haunting music and vivid colours while the water of the fountain that rose and fell and moved all around at the beat of the music combined with the colours in a fairytale effect. They spent hours gazing at the sight, sitting on the lawn, mesmerized. Towards the end of the show the mother turned to Stefano "My son you don't live in a city, you live in a fairytale. This place is so fabulous."

"Yes, this city mum won me at first glance. I've really put little to understand that here was where I had to stop."

"And I understand why," continued the mother.

"It is now time to go and get a beer in my favourite bar."

With this journey Giovanna could finally realize that her youngest son was fine. He had a successful bar full of people and the atmosphere among its employees was very friendly. He had created a place where people get together and loved to spend a few hours forgetting the problems of everyday life.

Her children were well. All of them. And now she knew that with certainty.

On their return journey home her mother said "Selin, you have made me the happiest mother in the world. The gift that you did to me and your father is invaluable and I have no words to tell you how much importance they had for me these nine days spent with the people I love most in the world, in places where they have chosen to spend their lives."

"Mum, believe me, is a gift that I wanted to do for myself. I needed to look at our family with your own eyes. In a way that Amaia, Stefano and Arianna know how to do instinctively but that I had lost the connection with, and you helped me to reconnect with all of us. Thanks mum."

"Thanks my dear daughter."

And with a wealth of experience completely new they went back to the place where it all began, -they returned home.
And Selin was happy to return in Matteo's arms.

CHAPTER XI

The following months went by quickly and smoothly; in the company of her family, of her old and new friends and this new relationship that made her feel a person inwardly rich, full and satisfied.

Those were the five months in which Selin could enjoy the warmth of her home, rediscover her mother and, therefore, rediscover herself. She was the same young women that before but free from those walls she had built around herself since been a teenager. She had been so focused on keeping others at a distance that she had not realized that she had kept at a distance herself. And probably the best part of those months was the feeling of lightness she felt within herself.

The worst part was knowing it would not last long: she saw her mother, although strong in spirit and with a sense of humour completely intact, feeling more and more tired day by day. It was hard for her to do any lifting at all. Cleaning the house would required her a huge effort and get up and down the stairs sucked her energy completely out of her body.

Her siblings had now left since a few weeks. Their life were calling them back: Stefano, having his own restaurant, he could not postpone his duties for a long time and Arianna had missed too many classes and so, as soon as things stabilized, they both took their flight back to their respective existences. Amaia, living in the same country, it was still very present in family life, but her priorities were to her own children and her own family. As for herself, Selin, did nothing but take care of the mother for the next two months. She relied on the fact that she had saved quite a bit in those years of only work and nothing else, and so she knew she could take the time to do nothing and slowly decide her future. She loved her job but she didn't want to leave her town, especially now that she had not only found her mother but also because she felt she was building something really important with Matteo. She had slowly started looking at potential jobs in her field in her region so that she didn't have to move to far, when one morning he received a call from her former employer. A cheerful and perky voice, that she had missed badly and that had for her a new job offer in the nearby town of Matera. Apparently, he did some research and noticed that Matera had a lot of potential in which he had decided to invest. Which meant opening a law firm that would cover the south and then open one in central Italy, while the firm in Milan would continued to cover the North and would have been the head office of the company. An ambitious project but since his clients portfolio was now more than solid he had decided to embark on a new challenge. What he needed to make his project succeed was a senior partner who he was familiar with and whom he trusted. Selin represented to him that person and he would not have taken 'no' for an answer. Selin agreed and soon her days saw her engaged in a new and exciting adventure. But her mornings and her evenings strictly belonged to her family. Every morning as she woke up, her mother would have been already waiting in the kitchen for breakfast with coffee and cookies laid out on the table while her father had already left to the countryside to take care of his garden, waking up at five in the morning, drinking a cup of milk and out of the house until lunch. One morning her mother asked her what she would miss most about her after her death. Although the word 'death' make her still shudder, her and her siblings had come to a total acceptance point of the reality in which they lived. Therefore, talk of her departure was no longer a taboo.

Selin didn't have to think about it for a long time before answering "what I will miss the most about you mum is your coffee."

When she realized that her mother's face clearly expressed utter confusion as a result of its response she added, "Mum, when you'll be here no more, what I will miss the most about you and that I will always remember about you is coffee. Ever since I was a kid, the drinking coffee has always been a time that belongs to you and you've always made it special. Drinking coffee is for you and everyone around you a moment of union. I always saw a lot of people when I was little, relatives, friends, neighbours, show up at the door at all times of the day to share a coffee with you. Which meant to sit here for hours talking and chatting around about husbands, household duties, comparing the prices between different supermarkets -about anything at all. But one thing never failed and it was the coffee. It was the way to welcome, to make the house pleasant in a way that would make everyone feel part of a family. I've never seen anyone in my entire life, walk through that door and feel uncomfortable or out of place or unwelcome. I remember I had to go and hide in the bedroom when I wanted to study, without telling anyone that I was in the house and you had to tell everyone that I had gone seen a friend. For me it was too much, really too much, overwhelmed me and I did not understand: but I do now! Despite my constant complaints about you drinking too much coffee every day, I do understand that a cup of coffee is your way to invite people to feel at ease and talk. Look at us now, somehow it has become also our time to communicate: the moment when I really feel connected with you and I can tell you anything. Always, every time I will be looking at a cup of coffee or smell coffee, wherever I am, I'll think of you, mum."

Her mother could not help from having tears in her eyes, overwhelmed with emotion, and to avoid bursting into tears she went to the sink to wash invisible cups or plates or something. And to break the tension she said "sure that you have always complained a lot about how much coffee I drank."

Selin laughed "Mum you drink way too much coffee and you've done nothing but lie to me about."

"I had to start to lie to you. You have forced me. It had become a matter of survival. Even if you were in Milan, each time I called you and you felt the voice of someone in the house you began to ask in that tone of a big boss *'mum how many coffees have you already drunk?'* I could imagine you vigorously shaking your head from side to side in disapproval. What have I always told you? You've always been too serious, too rigorous. Now I understand why you have chosen the law, so you have an excuse for your being so rigid."

"Okay mum, you're right. Totally! I agree and I admit I am the number one pain in the ass when it comes to judge and criticize whatever comes out of my sphere of understanding. You're right and I would not have ever noticed that if it had not been for your countless teasing. Let's enjoy this coffee and then let's get to clean this house, shall we?"

Five months and her alarm clock rang, she went into the kitchen and wondered why her mother was not there, intent to cook or wash or fold the clothes or anything. With a sense of nausea and suffocation she walked into her room and what she saw was her father, still wearing his pyjamas, sitting on a corner of the bed, staring into the eyes of a woman he loved for nearly forty years, with whom he has shared every day of his existence. A woman that now had her eyes closed, her pallor extremely pronounced and her chest that would not raised at the next breath. She was lying motionless, her hand wrapped in the hands of her husband. When her father became aware that someone else was in the room, he turned his head, looked at her without really seeing her and said only "she's gone".

The funeral was moving and a grand part of the town showed up to the function.   Her siblings arrived the same night of her death. Making those calls was for Selin one of the hardest things, probably the hardest, she had ever had to do in her life. As expected, her siblings could not contain themselves from bursting into tears. Their mother was gone, leaving behind a sense of overwhelming emptiness. They all felt so powerless in the face of so much pain. But all that pain was relieved when the day of her funeral, the family realized how much their mother had been loved. So many people had decided to go there for a final goodbye. Sitting respectfully for the duration of the function and many of them found the courage to express words of condolence, their deep affliction for a person who had the ability to be present in the lives of all of them. The most moving part was to walk together through the streets of the town, from the church to the cemetery, in strict silence. The only sound in the air was made by their feet pressing into the roads. There were no cars around nor kids playing, nor neighbours chatting between adjacent balconies. There was only the sound of footsteps of hundreds of people decided to take a last respectful greeting to a mother, a woman, a wife, and even more, a friend. His brother, his father and several uncles had decided that they wanted to carry on their shoulders the casket. They wanted to feel close to her one last time and their movement acted as guide to the rest of the town. The arrival at the cemetery was greeted by lots of flowers, of all types and all colours arranged all the way, from the entrance of the cemetery to the place where their mother was buried. And many lilac around her grave. It was no secret how her mother loved lilacs. Selin, her siblings and her father could not leave the cemetery until it was dusk, hours after everyone had started to return to their homes, to their lives. But they could not: in silence, standing looking at the cold grey headstone where the words "BELOVED UNTIL NOW AND FROM NOW" were a silent promise that everyone was going to keep.

They returned home and Amaia immediately began to prepare something to eat just to feel busy and keep her mind off the events of the past few days. The silence had become their new reality. It was overwhelming and painful but no one knew how to break it. No words seemed adequate. Their father went to his room only to return a few minutes later with a series of envelopes. Stopping by the side of the door, eyes fixed on those white envelopes firmly tight in his hands, "I don't know if there is a right time to do it but, kids, these are letters to each of you. Your mother has written them a month ago but made me promise not to say anything because she wanted you to read them only after her death. She made me promise to keep this from you until after the funeral." Arianna immediately left the chair by the fireplace, leaving the comfort of her brother's arms and rushed towards her father. She took the letters from his hand and gave it to her siblings, Amaia was the first to have her letter, Stefano was the next, Arianna took her aside and handed to Selin the last one.

Amaia immediately said "if you do not mind, I'd go home, my children ... I would like to read the letter with them." And without expecting any response, with tears in her eyes, she put the letter in her bag and left.

Arianna, however, could not help herself: she tore open the envelope and pulled out the letter and without hesitation began to read aloud the contents.

> *My dear Arianna,*
> *There are no words to describe how much I will miss you and how much I'm sick at the thought of soon not be able to enjoy more of your cheerful and noisy presence. I will miss our morning calls, where I had to stop whatever I was doing, because you wanted company on the way from home to school. For forty minutes, while you were on the bus, every morning you were going to describe me your previous day. And I wonder why there was always something cheerful and bizarre that it happened to you. Your voice has always rescued me a smile. I remember when you were only seven years ....*

Selin was unable to hear the rest. With the letter wrapped in her hands, she left the house and walked towards the country roads. The streets were still empty and silent, there was still a sense of sorrow in the air. She had walked that same path as when her mother had communicated for the first time that she was sick. But that night her heart was full of pain and her brain refused to even think of the word cancer. She was in total denial. That evening she failed to arrive in her private corner, that isolated part of the countryside overlooking a cliff and that at dusk was something magical. She had shared that special corner only with Matteo during her birthday.

Once again, she sat on the bench and lost her eyes in the infinite, the orange colour of the evening turned the horizon into flame. Selin took a deep breath and glanced at her hands. She could feel the weight of those words, still not pronounced, breaking through her heart. She looked at the envelope and noticed for the first time her name written in capital letters on one of the sides 'SELIN', simply her name. Another deep breath and she found the strength to open the envelope and extract the letter. The words began to dance before her moist and confusing eyes.

> *My dear Selin,*
> *It is so hard to find the right words. Among all of my children you are probably the most special. You were always my little adult.*

Always locked in her own world of well-defined rules and boundaries. I realize that our relationship has never been easy and this mainly because we are two different people, and sometimes we could not find a meeting point. In addition, your wanting to escape far away from us, away from your family, from your home-town has made me believe that you did not want my love. You have the same introverted and generous personality of your father. You both seem disinterested of the world around you when in fact you are just afraid to express the immense amount of love you have to give; most of all, you do not know how to express the feelings you hold in your heart and sometimes find it easier to repress your emotions under tons of strict rules. I remember how shy was your father when we had just met and I realized to late as some people could mistakenly exchange his shyness to disregard or even arrogance. You are the same! It took me a while to understand and, even more, to find a way to open a gap between us. I know I've made mistakes, many mistakes with you but I hope that the last few months spent together have earned your forgiveness.

I told you to be worried about you when you were just back from Milan because I was worried about you not to really be able to express yourself as rather your siblings can do. But, the reality is that I was afraid to leave before I could find a way to connect with you. But something happened: I am not sure what is it but in recent months I saw you more and more as yourself, more free, more confident, more sure of yourself. I saw you blossom and get rid of your chains. I saw you getting excited. I saw you having stronger views and not be frightened from expressing your emotions. And I felt the happiest woman in the world by the mere fact of having had the luck of witness those other layers of your personality. Never be afraid! Promise me. Live your life in the way that makes you happier. I know you will miss me but know that in one way or another I'm part of your life: I am in your memories, in your words, in your gestures. Do not be sad for me because thanks to you I know that I leave in the world a great and wonderful legacy: I leave you and your siblings in the world. I let the world enjoy what I have enjoyed over the years: the beauty of your soul and your kindness. I thank every day for having had the good fortune to have you in my life.

I have no advice to give you because you are perfect the way you are. You are my joy.

I love you!
Your mum

Selin, eyes wet with tears and a huge smile on her face, brought the letter close to her heart and lost herself again in the horizon. It was getting dark and the light breeze of the evening moved her hair. The sound of footsteps in the distance grab her attention and realized that someone was coming her way. That someone sat on the bench beside her. Matteo, hands still on the bench, staring at the vastness of the sky. He didn't look at her. He didn't touch her. But he sat down beside her. It was dark around them and Selin was still holding the letter in her hands, resting on her chest. With her heart swelling with hope and confidence, she knew that a wonderful new beginning it was revealing ahead of her. She rested her hand on Matteo's and with a smile Selin said, "Let's go home". And together they walked towards a future full of promises.

A deep thank you to my home-town, Bernalda, for inspiring this book. Even more, a huge thank you to my family, my parents and my sisters, for the daily support, the unconditional love always shown and, most of all, thank you for teaching me that the real family is the one that sticks together despite the difficulties of the everyday life... and we are family!

31686748R00089

Printed in Poland
by Amazon Fulfillment
Poland Sp. z o.o., Wrocław